Published by SO Nice Productions
Lakewood, Wa.
ISBN:979-8-9933579-0-4

SONOROUS CONSCRIPT
THE TRILOGY

TABLE OF CONTENTS

INTRODUCTION

In the near future, the world rediscovers something it was never meant to forget, the hidden power inside music. It is not a new discovery. Long before cities, screens, and machines, ancient tribes around the world already knew that rhythm could shape reality. From the heart of Africa to the islands of Samoa, music was more than art. It was energy. It was life.

Drums, chants, and melodies were not played for entertainment, they were used to awaken the strength sleeping inside people. Warriors could move faster, thinkers could see clearer, and healers could reach deeper, all through the pulse of sound.

As time passed, the world changed. Technology replaced tradition, and the harmony between humanity and music began to fade. The songs that once carried power became background noise. The leaders who guarded that wisdom, the elders, shamans, and maestros of spirit, were silenced, forgotten, or dismissed as myths.

Civilization grew louder, but humanity grew quieter. The connection that once tied heartbeats to rhythm slipped away.

Now that silence is breaking. Music is stirring again, alive in ways the world no longer understands. And when the first note returns, it will not just be heard, it will be felt.

The power that was lost is coming back.

And this time, it will not be forgotten.

DUBSTEP

The sunlight pouring through the tall windows of Harmonic Academy made the classroom glow. Rows of students sat in quiet anticipation as Mr. Anderson, their ever-energetic teacher, adjusted his Beatlocks and smiled like a man about to reveal a secret.

"Today, my young harmonizers, we dive into the wonders of dubstep," he announced, his voice carrying over the hum of excitement in the room. "This genre, with its pulsating beats and intricate bass drops, has the potential to unlock extraordinary abilities within you."

A few students sat up straighter. Others already had their Beatlocks in hand, eager to practice. But near the back of the room, Liam and Ava whispered to each other, more focused on their plans for the movie later than the lesson in front of them.

Mr. Anderson continued, oblivious for now. "Beginners in dubstep can manipulate vibrations to disrupt their surroundings, causing people to lose balance," he said, moving his hands to match his words. "Imagine the chaos you could create with just a well-timed bass drop."

A couple of students laughed quietly. The thought of tripping their friends during lunch with invisible waves of sound was almost too tempting. Meanwhile, Liam and Ava kept whispering, pretending to take notes while talking about what snacks they would sneak into the theater.

"Intermediate practitioners," Mr. Anderson went on, "can take it a step further, generating small earthquakes by harnessing the rhythmic energy of dubstep. Now, imagine the raw power at your fingertips."

The floor seemed to hum as his enthusiasm filled the air. But then his gaze sharpened.

"And then, my dear students," he said, his tone turning pointed, "experts in the art of dubstep can wield vibrations with such precision that they can walk through walls. In battle, they can shatter their opponents' eardrums with a single, controlled surge."

He paused. His eyes locked onto the two students still whispering in the back. The room fell silent.

"Do you two have something to share with the class?"
Ava froze mid-sentence. Liam straightened so fast his chair
squeaked against the tile. The vibrations in the room grew
heavier, like the sound itself was holding its breath.

They both shook their heads quickly. "No, sir," Liam said,
voice barely above a whisper.

Mr. Anderson's raised eyebrow softened into something that
was almost a smirk. The tension broke, and the subtle
vibration in the room faded away.

"Good," he said simply, motioning for them to stand. "Then
let's see how well you two were paying attention."

A few quiet "oohs" rippled through the class. Ava and Liam
exchanged a glance that was half nervous, half thrilled.
At the front of the room, Mr. Anderson handed them each
a pair of Beatlocks. "You'll take turns. Liam, defense. Ava,
offense."

The students leaned forward as he set the dubstep track.
The low thud of the opening beat pulsed through the room,
slow at first, then faster, deeper, until the floor began to
tremble.

Ava slid into a fighting stance. Her movements synced with
the rhythm, each step matching the tempo as the beat built
toward the drop. Liam raised his hands, bracing himself.

The bass hit.

Ava's eyes snapped open. She flipped backward over Liam in one fluid motion, landing behind him with perfect balance. The moment her feet touched down, she thrust her hands forward. A shockwave of vibration rippled through the air, sending Liam sliding across the floor with a surprised yelp.

The class gasped, then broke into applause and laughter. Even Liam couldn't help grinning as he got back to his feet. Mr. Anderson clapped, clearly impressed. "Excellent control, Ava. You've got the rhythm down. Liam, solid form under pressure. Both of you, well done."

He switched off the music, and the classroom settled again. Ava handed back her Beatlocks, a small proud smile on her face. Liam gave her a look that was half annoyed, half amused.

"Next time, maybe hold back a little?" he whispered as they walked back to their seats.

"You wish," Ava shot back with a grin.

The class erupted into quiet chatter again, the buzz of excitement still thick in the air. Outside, the bell rang, marking the end of another day at Harmonic Academy. Liam slung his backpack over his shoulder, and Ava adjusted her small crossbody purse. As they stepped into the hallway, students filled the corridors, showing off their powers. One trying to shatter glass with a low vibration, another forming a sound barrier just for fun. The school pulsed with energy, the rhythm of potential everywhere they looked.

For Ava and Liam, though, the school day was finally over.

"So, Ava, you ready for Let the Beat Build tonight?" Liam asked with an excited grin, his eyes reflecting anticipation.

Ava grinned back, her enthusiasm matching Liam's. "Absolutely! I've been looking forward to it all week. It's going to be epic! In the trailer, when the Jazz Bones absolute—"

Quickly, Liam stopped Ava with a mild look of frustration. "Ava! You know I don't like to watch the trailers! The trailers give away the whole movie. Don't tell me anything! I want to be surprised by it all!"

Deflated, Ava responded, "Oh, alright you tremble."

As they walked through the busy halls, weaving through the array of super-powered individuals, they continued discussing their plans for the evening. Liam, however, wanted to confirm the one detail that lingered in the back of his mind.

"Hey, did you get permission to go tonight?"

Ava chuckled, avoiding a direct answer. "Oh, you know, I have my ways."

Liam, not one to be easily swayed, persisted. "Ava, come on, did you, or didn't you?"

After a moment's hesitation, Ava sighed, admitting, "Okay, fine. My parents said I couldn't go. But don't worry, I have a plan to change their minds."

Liam raised an eyebrow, a mix of amusement and curiosity. "And what's this genius plan?"

Ava grinned mischievously. "Extra chores, my friend. If I help out more at home, they'll have no choice but to let me go. It's foolproof."

Liam chuckled, shaking his head. "I knew I'd get roped into your schemes sooner or later."

Ava laughed. "You love it, and you know it."

With a playful roll of his eyes, Liam agreed to help Ava with her extra chores. They continued walking home as they chatted about their plans and laughed at the day's events. As they walked, Ava could see her brother Oscar talking to Elijah.

Oscar was a little older than Ava and more advanced in his Bass Masters studies, the art of dubstep. Ava and Oscar were very close, but they couldn't be more different. The fun-loving Ava unintentionally activated her abilities when she was just twelve, at a dubstep concert. Oscar, on the other hand, discovered his abilities while working hard, experimenting with dubstep frequencies. Even though Oscar gained his powers later in life, he quickly outclassed Ava. This, however, was great for her, as she had always been able to lean on him for guidance in advancing her skills and strengthening her techniques.

Elijah worked closely with Oscar. He was a physics prodigy and unlocked his ability while experimenting. Oscar studied and experimented with frequencies, and Elijah found a way to manipulate the frequency of vibrations to create unique effects. That was the main reason so many students begged to be tutored by him. Once again, Ava was able to benefit since Oscar and Elijah were practically always together.

"Wave, Freq, what are you guys up to?" Oscar's nickname was Wavelength while Elijah's was Frequency. Once you mastered all the beginner techniques, you were assigned a nickname. The instructors who watched your performance chose the name based on your powers. Bass Masters all learned the same techniques, but every person was different, and their powers fluctuated.

Oscar looked over and smiled when he realized who it was. "What's up lil sis!?"

Elijah greeted Ava. "Hey little Soundwave!"

Embarrassed, Ava quickly responded. "Hey, you know I'm still a rookie. I won't get any nicknames until I get all my moves down."

Elijah laughed. "Oh come on, with all the extra training you've been getting from me and Wave, you'll have them down in no time."

Liam chipped in, "No kidding, she's already the best in our class. You should have seen what she did to me today!"

Oscar asked, "Ava, you know you're not supposed to spar outside of class. It's dangerous!"

Liam grabbed Oscar's attention again. "Oh no, this was in class, in front of everyone!"

"Wait, what?" asked Oscar. Ava diverted her eyes, embarrassed by the story, while Liam continued.

"Yeah, we got caught whispering in class. Mr. Anderson had us come up to prove we were paying attention. Ava nailed this Backflip Bass Drop and hit me with the Vibrogenesis!"

Shocked, Oscar said, "But that's an intermediate move. Who did you learn…" He stopped, realizing the answer. His eyes flicked to Elijah, who was suddenly looking away. They all started laughing while Oscar yelled, "Freq!!"

Laughing back, Elijah defended himself. "Come on, Wave, she's so talented. In my opinion, she's mastered Resonance Awareness and Hyper-Reflex Harmonics. She just wanted a taste of what's next."

Oscar, impressed, said, "Oh she's mastered them, has she? Okay. Ava, what can you do with Resonance Awareness?"

Quickly, Ava answered, as confident as ever. "Resonance Awareness is vibrational perception. It allows the user to enhance their senses to perceive their surroundings through vibrations. This can help detect hidden objects, people, or materials."

Clapping his hands, Elijah cheered, "Yeah! See, she's got this down!"

Pleased with her response, Ava smiled brightly.

Oscar, being the supportive big brother, complimented her before adding, "That was almost perfect! Don't forget, while using Resonance Awareness, you can also sense the emotional state of others through their vibrational frequencies. With all the work I do with frequencies, I thought you'd remember that for sure."

Appreciating the constructive criticism, Ava thanked the two of them and promised she would keep practicing.

Oscar reminded her, "It's fine to practice advanced moves. Just remember you have to master the entry techniques before you can advance."

"I'll get a lot of practice tonight at the movies."

Confused, Oscar said, "I thought Mom and Dad said you couldn't go tonight."

Liam replied sarcastically, "She thinks that if we do some extra chores around the house, they might change their minds."

Oscar laughed. "They never change their minds!" Then he thought for a moment. He was supposed to wash Dad's car today, but he had been busy with a discovery. Maybe this was the perfect opportunity.

Oscar became serious. "Actually, that might work. I overheard Dad say he wished he had time to wash the car, but he was too busy. I bet if you had that thing cleaned by the time he got home, he'd let you go."

Refilled with hope, Ava asked, "And what about Mom?"

"That's easy," replied Oscar. "Go with the two-for-one. Mom's been wanting Dad to mow the lawn, but he hasn't had time. If you mow the lawn, you'd make both of them happy in one shot."

Quick as a whip, Ava announced, "Thank you, Oscar, that's brilliant! If we just mow the lawn, I won't have to wash the car! That will make them both happy! Thank you!"

Oscar tried to rebut, but Ava hugged him tight, squeezing the argument out of him. Then she hugged Elijah before she and Liam walked off. Knowing what Oscar was trying to do, Elijah stared at him.

Oscar laughed. "What, man?"

Elijah laughed back. "Smooth, dude."

The two of them chuckled as they walked toward their offices, eager to return to their research.

DISCOVERY

Oscar and Elijah walked down a large hallway as they continued their discussion.

"How long did it take Ava to learn Vibrogenesis?" Oscar asked.

With a serious tone, Elijah replied, "I only showed her once. I told her it was too advanced, and she wouldn't be able to pick it up just yet. Then she hit me in the feels, told me I was like a brother to her, and asked me to show her once. I agreed to show her so I could prove how difficult it was. I figured I would show her, she would see how difficult it was, and stop asking until later. But like I said, I showed her once, and she mimicked my moves perfectly. It was insane. I have never seen anything like it."

Before responding, Oscar had to sit with that information. Did Ava just copy his moves as Elijah said, or was it something else? Oscar had always been curious about Ava's abilities. Oscar's talents seemed to depend on his work and his research. In contrast, Ava appeared to naturally sync with dubstep effortlessly. Ava did put in the hours, studying and practicing, but she seemed to yield better results than anyone else. Another proud smile crept onto his face as he looked up at the large door in front of them.

To the eye, it appeared to be a large door without a doorknob, a window, a keypad, or a lock. It was just a large door, made out of stone. Only those who had learned vibrology, the vibrational language, could open the door. The secured doors in this facility had several layers of security. The keys to gaining entry included tactical vibration, infrasonic sound waves, ultrasonic sound waves, and biological vibrations.

Elijah began the process of opening the door. The first step was to lower his heart rate to exactly sixty beats per minute. Secondly, this door required an infrasound not heard by the human ear. Lastly, Elijah reached out and touched the door. With his hands, he made a beat on the stone that was specific to this door and this door only.

After all three levels of security were met, the door began to open, revealing an incredible, state-of-the-art lab. As Elijah walked through the threshold, he let out a low hum in a nonchalant manner. This was the fourth and last security measure. The hum had to meet the correct frequency. Failure to do this would set off a silent alarm followed by hundreds of staff and security. It was something Oscar had learned the hard way, which was why Elijah decided to open the door.

Elijah jumped right back into their research. "Ok. As you know, I have been working on this for a while now. The reason I have brought you in is because I think you could offer a fresh perspective that could prove invaluable."

"Thanks again for bringing me in on this! When I first heard about your research, I began dabbling in the study of vibration which led me to discover my abilities. You are legendary in my book, and I can't wait to learn from you and expand beyond these walls!"

Elijah jokingly dismissed Oscar's compliments. "Oh, come on, you know that wisdom is just experience applied well. Your eagerness to innovate is just as crucial to this project. Let's give this another try. Our goal is to create a device that allows us to combine our vibration abilities with technology. The device should then distribute the vibrations to create a wide range of subtle vibrations that we will then use as a form of detection."

Oscar suddenly realized he did not know the reason for building such a device. "Is this a project you came up with on your own?"

Deep in thought, Elijah replied in a mundane voice, "No, I was asked if such a device could be created. The idea seemed possible, and I am never one to turn down a challenge." He grabbed a pen and started writing quickly in a pad, as if afraid to forget his thought.

Oscar asked, "Why don't we use a combination of infrasonic and ultrasonic sound waves? We could use the same sound waves we used to get in here. The ultrasonic sound waves could be used for precision in close-range situations. The infrasonic sound waves could be utilized for a wider range. We could just use our abilities in real time to fine-tune and control the waves."

Elijah stopped writing to think. "Interesting concept. Ultrasonic waves do offer high resolution ideal for pinpointing objects, while infrasonic waves cover broader areas efficiently. But we must ensure balance. If we use too much power, we could have unintended consequences. How do you propose we mitigate this?"

Elijah, full of hope, watched as he realized Oscar was in the zone. With every second that went by, Elijah stood still, afraid that one distraction could pull Oscar away from his train of thought.

"Perhaps we could integrate a feedback mechanism into the device. It could continuously monitor the environment and adjust the intensity and vibrations accordingly. Our abilities could augment this feedback loop, ensuring precise control."

"Oscar! You are onto something. A feedback mechanism! We would need a few sensors capable of detecting changes in the environment. It would need to analyze the data to make the proper adjustments. The scans would start with an infrasonic wave to obtain a general area, then change to an ultrasonic wave as we got closer to whatever we were detecting. The user input would ensure the device was always working properly, giving us the ability to manually override at a moment's notice, and we could use our powers to enhance sensitivity and precision."

Jumping in right where Elijah left off, Oscar added, "Yes! A user-friendly interface is essential. The user could set the parameters such as the size and the material for the target object, and the device could adjust settings accordingly."

"This is a great foundation, Oscar, great work. Let's get started putting these concepts into practice. I suggest we start working on that feedback mechanism."

"Sounds good to me, man. Do you know what we will be using the device for? I know you said it was for detection, but detecting what?"

"I honestly have no idea. I was asked to make this device, but I never inquired what it would be used for. Let's cross that bridge when we get there. This is going to be huge!"

As the two brilliant young men got to work, Oscar could not stop thinking about the purpose of the machine. A device that could detect objects. If he knew the purpose, he could invent with certain requirements in mind. Was this going to be stationary equipment, or should it be mobile? Would it be for commercial use or private sector use only? Was there a budget they should aim for? All of these questions lingered in Oscar's mind. Even with all these questions buzzing in his head, Oscar kept them to himself, not wanting to disturb Elijah, who appeared to have a renewed excitement for the project.

Unexpectedly, the door to the office opened, and standing there was Zara, Oscar's older sister and the eldest sibling of the Rodriguez family. Zara was just as sweet as her other two siblings, but she was very advanced in the art of dubstep. Currently, Zara worked as a sound engineer and producer, specializing in manipulating and enhancing sonic elements. Her occupation provided a unique platform to merge Bass Masters abilities with cutting-edge audio technology, creating innovative and transformative auditory experiences. She could harmonize vibrations, creating a calming influence on the environment. This was why Oscar had recommended consulting her on the project. Elijah did not hesitate to follow that advice.

"Boys! What's all the commotion? Usually, when I listen in on your vibes, all I hear is theoretical brainstorming. Today seemed a bit different, I had to come and check it out in person."

Elijah, quick to give credit, said, "Wavelength has made a melodic turning point in our research. Essentially, he suggested creating a device that can emit both infrasonic and ultrasonic sound with user controls, equipped with a feedback mechanism to ensure we do not have any inadvertent environmental activity."

With her expertise in balancing vibrations and calming the environment, Zara became curious. "How would a device like this work exactly? Even with my abilities, I don't think I could put into words how I feel what the environment tells me. I can just sense things, but nothing tangible."

"Simple," said Oscar. "We first create a sensor that can scan everything we know of—temperature, density, oxygen, etc. Before using the device, we would scan the immediate area, and if our sensors detected any change while using the device, it would automatically adjust to stop that change."

"And with the ability to manually control the device in real time, we could even reverse the inadvertent change. Dependent on the proficiency of the user, of course." After speaking, Elijah gave a nod to Oscar to once again acknowledge it was his idea. "Harmony, your brother outdid himself with this one."

"That sounds amazing, guys. When do you think this device will be ready?"

"I am not sure," responded Elijah.

Trying to get his questions answered, Oscar joined in. "We would need to decide on a few things before we can move too far forward. For instance, if this device is going to be mobile, we will need to ensure that all our sensors are small but strong enough to detect farther than we can already detect. The problem with compact devices is heat distribution. They will always have a heating issue, which we cannot begin to fix until we encounter it. Also, we do not know what this device will be used for yet. Once we do, we can ensure the device can detect that without a doubt. Other materials can be added as production continues."

As Oscar spoke, he could see Elijah deep in thought. Right away, Oscar knew his plan to get Elijah on the same page worked.

"I'm sorry, you two. It seems I will need to get some of those questions answered before we continue. Oscar, can we pick this back up tomorrow?"

"Of course, Freq. Great work today!"

"Oh, and can you two keep this between us? I was told to keep this research to myself. I begged to get Wave onto the project, and I have not even mentioned that we have consulted you on this, Harmony."

"You already know it, Freq, my lips are sealed."

"As far as I'm concerned, I know nothing. Additionally, I have no interest in sharing any information about this device. No offense. I believe you two have great intentions, and to hear that your initial project will have environmental protections is promising. However, if anyone decided to create this device without the protections you plan to put in place, well, that could be dangerous. You two must keep this close to the chest until you come up with a working prototype of that feedback mechanism you mentioned."

They were all in agreement as they left the lab together. All three were happy for different reasons. Oscar was excited about helping his esteemed colleague with a breakthrough. Elijah was eager to tell his superiors about the progress. And Zara was elated that the youth were finally thinking about the environment.

Elijah made his way to the third floor of the building and continued left and right past offices until he reached the corner office where his boss was diligently working. As Elijah walked past the long glass window, he rubbed the nonverbal announcement strip. These strips had been installed a few years ago to reduce noise pollution in the office. Instead of knocking and asking to come in, someone could simply swipe a braille phrase, and anyone who could interpret the vibration would understand. Without looking up, Nathan Turner waved Elijah inside. Nathan appeared busy typing away at his keyboard.

In walked Elijah, welcomed by a "Juuuusssst onnnnnne seeeeecoooond… and done." Nathan finished by hitting the enter key louder than the rest to signify he was done. As he finally looked up, Nathan saw Elijah at the door. Nathan stood quickly with a smile, glanced through the windows of his office to see if anyone was nearby, then shook Elijah's hand firmly before motioning for him to sit. He gave one more look outside before closing the door and returning behind his desk.

Nathan then asked, "Elijah, what brings you in today?"

"Well sir, I've been giving our recent progress a lot of thought. When we initially embarked on this project, it was about creating a device that could harness vibrations to detect objects at great distances. But now, with the breakthrough my partner and I have made, I can't shake this nagging feeling about the real intent behind our work." Relieved to finally say it, Elijah looked to his superior for answers.

"Ah, Elijah, it's good to see you're contemplating the broader implications of our research. And what is this about a breakthrough? I would love to hear more." There was an awkward pause as Nathan expected a debrief and Elijah was still waiting for his question to be answered.

"You know what, where are my manners? You came in with questions. You can fill me in later. What exactly is on your mind?"

Grateful to stay on topic, Elijah cut to the chase. "Well, Nathan, I can't help but wonder about the intended applications of this device. What precisely are we aiming to detect? It would be good to know so we could ensure the device is optimized for said objects. I was also curious who would be using this device and for what purpose."

"Those are all pertinent questions. Regarding the purpose, let's just say it's geared toward identifying specific targets, people of interest, if you will. I would like the device to be mobile, as the user may need to search beyond their starting location if the target is out of reach."

"I appreciate you being candid with me. Forgive me if I am somewhat skeptical. Identifying specific targets might raise some questions about privacy and ethics we have not discussed. The emphasis on mobility hints at operational requirements beyond mere surveillance. Is there more you can share about the intended use?"

"I understand your concerns, but there are certain sensitive matters I am not at liberty to disclose. Trust that our work serves a vital purpose, and we must proceed with caution."

"Proceed with caution..." Elijah repeated. "That statement is specifically what worries me, Nathan. I want to believe in the greater good, but I can't shake this feeling of unease. What if our creation is misused or exploited for nefarious purposes?"

"We have protocols in place to prevent such occurrences, Elijah. But I need your unwavering commitment to see this project through. Your expertise is invaluable, and I trust you'll prioritize our objectives above all else."

"Of course, Nathan. I'm dedicated to advancing our research, but I hope you understand my reservations. I'll continue to work diligently, but I urge you to consider the broader ramifications of our endeavors."

The conversation concluded with Elijah feeling torn between his dedication to the project and his ethical concerns, while Nathan remained steadfast in pursuit of the objectives. Despite their uneasy exchange, both recognized the gravity of their roles in shaping the future of their creation.

"Now, unless you have any further questions, can you discuss this breakthrough with me?"

Elijah decided to trust Nathan, the same person who had guided his success so far, and explained Oscar's theory. Full of excitement, Nathan urged Elijah and Oscar to start making a prototype as soon as possible. Before leaving Nathan's office, Elijah was told to keep this conversation between the two of them. Elijah agreed, though he did not feel much better than when he walked in. He decided to head home for some much-needed rest.

TAKEN

Back at the Rodriguez household, Ava had finished mowing the lawn, Liam placed all the pulled weeds into the yard waste bin, and Oscar was drying the newly cleaned family car.

"Ava, I think now is the time to ask."

Exhausted, Ava agreed and asked, "Do you think I should ask my mom or dad?"

After a second of thought, Liam suggested, "Your dad! Wasn't mowing the lawn his chore? Maybe he'll be so happy you did something for him, he'll say yes."

Ava argued, "He might allow me, but my mom was the one who originally told me no. If I go around her to ask him, she'll ground me."

While the two young Bass Masters talked it over, they overheard Oscar. "Hey Mom, I'm done washing the car! I'm going to take Ava and Liam to the theatre if you're still ok with it?"

As Oscar yelled that into the house, Ava and Liam looked at each other in confusion.

Without stepping out of the house, their mother hollered back, "Yes, of course, great work everyone! Stay safe and stay together!"

"Will do, Mom!" Oscar looked at his sister and said, "Let's go!"

Ava burst out, "What just happened!"

With a smirk, Oscar revealed his secret. "I agreed to clean the car and chaperone the two of you last week for you to go." He opened his arms, closed his eyes, and waited for a huge hug from his sister. After a few moments, he peeked one eye open to see a squinty-eyed Ava.

"Earlier today, you told me to wash the car and mow the lawn and maybe Mom would let me go!"

Oscar laughed. "I thought you might remember that! Man, you are smart, Ava. I'm proud of you. But come on, you can't blame me for trying, can you?"

Ava let out a small laugh. "Oh, I can blame you, but I'll let it slide since you did volunteer to take me."

Ava, Liam, and Oscar headed into the city for the premiere of a movie. As the group settled into their seats at the theatre, Ava's anticipation grew. She had been looking forward to seeing *Let the Beat Build* for weeks. The documentary promised to explore the origins of dubstep, a genre of electronic dance music she was deeply passionate about. Ava couldn't wait to immerse herself in the history and culture of the music she loved.

Once they arrived, they took their seats. Ava had been to the theatre many times, so it was confusing when she saw the entire back row roped off and reserved. The group, now seated, enjoyed some light conversation before the movie began. Ava continuously looked back to see if anyone was going to occupy the reserved seats, but no one came.

Eventually, the lights dimmed, and everyone quieted down. Ava looked back again, and still, the rear seats were empty. Her eyes widened with wonder as the screen came to life, pulsating with vibrant colors and electrifying visuals. The thumping bass reverberated through the theatre, sending shivers down her spine. It was like being transported to another world, one where music held the power to move mountains and transcend boundaries.

Ava was enjoying the spectacle, but she was distracted as she finally noticed people slipping into the reserved seats. It was eerie to watch the group sneak into the row without being detected. Her curiosity turned to apprehension. Who were these people, and what were they doing here?

Everyone in the group was masked. It was something she had never seen before, and she became concerned. The masked individuals wore sleek, form-fitting attire that seemed to blend with the shadows, colored only in matte black and dark gray.

Ava nudged Oscar, who was fully engaged in the performance. He looked over and noticed the concern in his sister's eyes.

"What's wrong?" he asked.

Ava replied, "Don't be obvious, but look at the people in the back. Have you ever seen people like that before?"

Oscar took a quick look and returned his gaze to Ava. He remembered seeing similar outfits in a briefing at work, but he couldn't place it. In an attempt to calm his sister, Oscar said, "We are literally at a movie theatre. Surely those people were checked in just like us."

"Then why are they wearing masks?" Ava asked.

Oscar looked back one last time. His silence gave him away. He had no answer, and his attempts to calm Ava only pulled him into her worry.

Without warning, the movie cut off and a woman appeared on the screen. Ava's heart pounded as dread washed over her. The woman wore the same attire as the strangers in the back row. They had suspected something earlier, but now they knew. Something terrible was about to happen.

Liam groaned, "Ah, come on, what is this?"

In preparation for the worst, Oscar pulled out a pair of flex-wrap Beatlocks and passed them to Ava. She looked down at what she was being handed, then back up at him. He urged her to take them, and she did.

Flex-wrap Beatlocks were essentially portable Beatlocks. Designed thin enough to fit in a pocket, once placed on the user's forehead they activated and wrapped around the head, encapsulating the ears. The Beatlocks were programmable to trigger absolute noise cancellation, known as A.N.C., and play an endless track of the user's preferred music.

Oscar carrying an extra pair for Ava meant he expected trouble. Ava slipped them into her pocket and returned her attention to the screen.

The woman spoke. "Good evening, Bass Masters. We must perform an auditory test of the theatre speakers. This will only take a minute."

The speakers let out a speedy drum solo, then an electric guitar and screaming vocals. Metal music blasted through the theatre, strange for a Bass Master venue. The music shifted again. A loud beep sounded, and one seat illuminated. A person in the back was escorted away. Then the music turned to country until another seat illuminated. This continued, as people were led out without explanation.

When the music changed to hip hop, Ava felt a strange sensation. It was familiar yet deeply unsettling. She couldn't tell if it was the bizarre situation or something else. Then her seat illuminated.

A stranger grabbed Ava's arm. His voice was strict and low. "Come with me."

Oscar started to rise, but the stranger stopped him. "No. Stay in your seat until the test is concluded."

Oscar froze, but his mind raced. Ava was equipped with Beatlocks. She could protect herself if she had to. Reluctantly, he sat back down.

Ava was escorted out while Oscar watched helplessly. The music kept shifting genres as more people were taken.

Around him, whispers spread. The music drowned out most words, but he caught fragments. Some thought the chosen seats had faulty speakers and people were being given refunds. Others believed the removals were tied to pirating the movie online.

Finally, the test ended and the film resumed. Oscar knew none of the rumors were true. Ava wasn't a pirate, and her speakers weren't broken. She had been taken.

Oscar and Liam rushed out to the lobby. Groups of frantic families were demanding answers. Staff members, equally confused, insisted no test had been announced, and no one had been escorted out. Oscar's heart sank.

He bolted outside to the parking lot but saw nothing unusual. Liam caught up, his voice trembling. "Where did they take Ava?"

A commotion erupted at the back of the building. There was no access from the front. The two ran back inside, forcing their way through the growing crowd.

Oscar could tell from the vibrations that someone was using Bass. He pulled on his Beatlocks and activated the A.N.C. to focus. But as he reached for the frequency, the vibrations vanished. Ava's presence was gone.

Panic surged through him. He shoved through the last of the crowd and burst outside, just in time to see four black vehicles speeding away. A fifth SUV lay destroyed, flipped on its side.

"AVA!" Oscar screamed, sprinting to the wreck. He checked the front seats, then the back—empty.

Frustration boiled over. He screamed, unleashing a powerful vibrational force field known as Sonic Constructs.

The blast shook the air. Liam, just stepping outside, was thrown back into the building by the sheer force.

Oscar's eyes swept the area again, but there was no sign of Ava. His sister, his best friend, was gone.

UNEXPECTED

Oscar, in a state of shock and complete loss, stood there. His mind racing a mile a minute, he was brought back to reality by Liam pulling on his shirt. Oscar disabled the A.N.C. and told Liam they needed to get to the lab. Oscar and Liam made their way there. On the way, Oscar called Elijah and asked him to meet at the lab.

Confused by the late phone call, Elijah's first instinct was to question the motive. But being a close friend of Oscar, he could hear the concern in his voice and knew there was a legitimate reason. Without hesitation, Elijah agreed to meet, got out of bed, and quickly made his way to the lab.

Once inside, Oscar was shocked to find signs that someone had been there. The lab was more cluttered than when they had left it that morning. Liam was still in shock from losing Ava. What condition was she in? How distraught would their parents be? With all these questions floating around in his head, Oscar was beginning to lose focus. But amidst the chaos and confusion, one thing remained clear: Ava was out there, and he would stop at nothing to find her. With every fiber of his being, Oscar vowed to bring his sister home safe and sound, no matter the cost. He was frantically looking around the lab when Elijah finally walked in.

"Freq, someone has been in here! It looks like they were making something."

"I know, Bass, it was me. After I met with Nathan, I planned on going home to get some rest. But I was too excited about your concepts and decided to get started."

Oscar realized Elijah was pulling something on wheels, covered with a jacket. Elijah dragged the device into the middle of the room and uncovered it. The machine was triquetra in shape and encased in brass, with a detachable power source on the backside.

Impressed, Oscar asked, even though he assumed it was the exact device they had conceived that morning, "What is this?"

Excited to explain, Elijah said, "This machine is exactly what you thought up this morning. Most of the components already existed. I just had to amplify the range and impose a structural design that would allow us to make contact with the ground. After that, I dismantled a few other devices and repurposed their sensors to compose the feedback mechanism. I was able to connect the mechanism to both the infrasonic and ultrasonic wave emitters pointed toward the ground. This third point of the triquetra contains the feedback mechanism." Nearly out of breath, Elijah looked at Oscar. He expected excitement on Oscar's face, but saw only panic.

"How do you control it?" Oscar asked.

"What's wrong, Bass? I just told you I made your concepts a reality, and you don't seem nearly as excited as I thought you would be."

"I just need to use it now. Please, Freq. Tell me how to use this thing."

"We can't use it yet, man. We still have to work with Zara. We have to make sure the feedback mechanism works."

"I don't have time for that. Someone just took my sister! I need to find her now!"

The gravity of the situation instantly hit Elijah. His heart skipped a beat. It was like all the oxygen in his body had been sucked out. He knew Oscar was talking about Ava, the sweet young girl, his kid sister. Elijah's mind went to moments they had shared, working together, laughing, and training.

Without another word, Elijah hooked up the device to a monitor. It powered on. "I'll get it running. There's no time to give you a crash course. I'm not even sure if it will work yet. What will we be looking for?"

"There were five—well, four—black SUVs leaving south from the theatre. I'm pretty sure Ava destroyed the fifth one."

"She destroyed it!?"

"Yeah, a strange group took her from the theatre. I slipped her a Beatlock before she was taken. I'm assuming when they were loading people into the cars, she fought back. By the time I made it to her, they were already leaving. I don't know why they took her or what they want with her. I know with her abilities, she wouldn't just stop fighting. But her vibe was gone. Before I got to her, it just disappeared."

As Oscar finished, the device began doing what it was designed to do. Rods shot into the ground. Infrasonic waves pulsed through the floor, and the building began to shake.

Elijah turned to the monitor. "The feedback mechanism doesn't appear to be working. Right, I was supposed to scan the environment before activating the device. Ok, I'll control it manually!"

Oscar hit a few keys and two circular panels opened. This exposed the visible sound waves being created and amplified by the device. He reached his hands inside and let out a painful yell.

"Freq!"

"I'm fine!" he hollered. "It's just more intense than I imagined. It's amazing, Bass! I can feel and see everything. For miles, I can see everything!" The shaking of the walls stopped. No damage seemed to have been done to the building.

"Look for my sister, Freq!"

"There! Four SUVs, headed west on State Route 22 at high speeds. Looks like each is full."

"Which one has Ava inside!?"

"It's not that detailed. I'd need to switch to the infrasonic wave, but at this distance it wouldn't reach. I can't hold on much longer, Oscar. My hands—"

"Check the monitor. You see where they are?"

"Yeah, I got it. You can let go!"

Elijah released the field and fell back. His hands shook violently and uncontrollably. Groaning, he stared at them while Oscar powered down the device.

"We have to get on the road and continue tracking before they split up or get out of range."

Just then, the lab doors opened. Nathan stormed in. "What is going on in here!?" His eyes swept the room and landed on Liam, whom he didn't know. He started to question him, but then his gaze froze on the machine.

"It works, Nathan," Elijah said, breaking the silence. He glanced back at his hands, which were returning to normal. "We need to take it with us. Oscar's sister is in danger."

Nathan snapped out of his trance and glared at Elijah. "Take it with you? This device will not leave this room. And what is this about Oscar's sister being in danger?"

Oscar stepped in. "Nathan, Sir, I was at the theatre with Ava and Liam. Masked people came in. They said they were doing an auditory test, playing all kinds of music. Seats began to light up, including Ava's. They took her, and when I checked the staff, no one knew what was happening. I chased them, saw one SUV destroyed, but four others took off with her."

"One destroyed SUV? What do you mean?"

"When they started taking people, I gave Ava a pair of Beatlocks so she could protect herself."

"You gave an unlicensed user Beatlocks!?"

"Yes, it was an emergency! I think they tried forcing people into the SUVs and Ava fought back. By the time I went to her last location, she was gone, and I couldn't sense her vibe."

"I cannot believe you would do something like that. When I let you into this project, I thought you had better decision-making skills. Effective immediately, you are no longer on this project. Do you understand?"

"Sir, did you just hear what I said!? My sister and a group of people were kidnapped from a theatre in our city. And why didn't you even seem surprised when I told you about it?"

"This isn't the first time something like this has happened. We're dealing with it. That does not excuse your poor judgment. You and this boy will leave the lab now or I'll have you both arrested."

In disbelief, Oscar looked to Elijah. Elijah spoke up, "Sir, if we could first look for—"

"There is no first. You two leave now!"

Oscar and Liam left quickly, leaving Elijah with Nathan.

"What a night," Nathan muttered coldly, as if only annoyed. "Elijah, I know you have been working with Zara on this project. While I don't appreciate dishonesty, I understand your drive. That is why I allowed you to bring in the two Martinez siblings. From now on, you will report to me on any issue regarding this device. You will no longer discuss the project with Oscar. Do you understand?"

"But Sir, without Oscar——"

"Do you understand?"

"Yes, Sir."

As Elijah watched Oscar and Liam leave under Nathan's stern gaze, he felt torn between loyalty to his friend and obedience to his superior. The weight of the situation hung heavy. Nathan's dismissal of Ava's kidnapping gnawed at him.

He nodded reluctantly, but inside he burned with determination. He would not abandon Oscar, and he would not let Ava vanish. Whatever Nathan was hiding, Elijah would uncover it.

The night had only just begun, and the path ahead promised danger, betrayal, and revelations. As Elijah turned back to the device, he took a deep breath. Ava's fate hung in the balance. The stakes were higher than ever, and failure was not an option.

A few hours ago…

FRIENDSHIP

Mrs. Layden asked the class, "All right, who can come up to the front of the class and explain the capabilities of those powered by Pop?" In the middle of the class, one hand shot up above the rest, wiggling in excitement. Mrs. Layden looked around for anyone else. She did not pass over the hand out of annoyance, however she wanted to give someone else the opportunity to answer.

Mrs. Layden looked at a shy little girl who was sitting in the front of the room. This girl's name was Rachel. She was a very pretty girl, taller than the rest of the class. She had sandy brown hair that was long and curly. Rachel had beautiful brown eyes and was very smart. Mrs. Layden noticed that Rachel was always watching and paying attention; however, she did not speak out often.

"Rachel, how about you come up and answer my question?" Rachel looked down at her notes, as if she didn't know the answer already. She stood up and walked to the front of the class. Without hesitation, she began to speak.

"Those who are super powered by Pop music are called Singing Sirens. These powers draw inspiration from the infectious and captivating nature of Pop music, providing individuals with the charisma and influential abilities to connect with others, captivate audiences, and navigate social situations with charm and popularity, which is why we are considered sirens. Competent wielders of Pop can be extremely persuasive. Experts can gain an instant rapport which can be used to gain a strategic advantage in battle."

"Great job, Rachel. You are perfectly right. Go ahead and take your seat." The class watched as Rachel sat down. The children were all impressed with how she was able to give such an amazing answer. Rachel rarely talked in class. Most just assumed she was either shy or wasn't paying attention.

Mrs. Layden continued teaching the class. "Singing Sirens can be very powerful, however we have been silenced as people in the past have ruined our credibility. Any time a Siren is seen wearing their Beatlocks, others immediately equip their A.N.C. as a precaution. In the past, our people have taken advantage of humanity as they had no defense against us. With this absolute noise cancellation, we are no longer able to take the primary role in battle. We must learn other ways to defend and protect ourselves."

As she finished her sentence, the class bell rang and they were dismissed. Rachel started to walk toward the door before she was cut off by Jessica Parker.

"I had no idea you were so smart, Maestro!" Jessica was an intermediate student just like Rachel. Given the fact the two had never talked, Rachel was surprised Jessica even knew her name. Jessica opened the classroom door for Rachel.

"Thank you, Princess." Since Jessica used her nickname, Rachel decided to use Jessica's.

"Ugh, please don't call me that." The two of them continued walking down the hall. "I was so excited to get my new name when I learned all my basic techniques. After all, I had to practice so hard to learn Pop Pulse Projection, and it felt like an eternity. When I finally took my test, I was told I performed so elegantly, like a Princess. They wound up calling me Pop Princess. I was devastated. There are so many cool names out there, and I got Pop Princess."

"Pop Princess is a great name!"

"Easy for you to say, Muse Maestro! Your name is both strong and elegant." Rachel was quite speechless. On the same day, Jessica had begun talking to her and now she was complimenting her. The way Jessica described her nickname as being strong and elegant, it was almost as if she had put some thought into it prior to this conversation.

"Thank you, Jessica." Rachel was deep in thought. What was going on? Why was she talking to me now? It couldn't be for the simple fact that I answered that one question in class today.

"I bet you're wondering why I am talking to you all of a sudden." Rachel quickly looked up at Jessica as if she had listened to her thoughts. "I always knew you were smart. I remember hearing about how you impressed the instructors when you completed your beginner's demonstration. I just thought you were shy. After I saw you get up today and address the class, I realized you were not just shy. You just didn't have anyone to talk to. When I first came to this academy, I felt the same way. I kept to myself and I didn't really branch out much. But then, I made one friend and it had a snowball effect. I would like us to be friends. What do you think?"

Rachel was elated to hear Jessica say this. In all her time at the Sound Academy, she had not made one friend. Making friends was not Rachel's strong suit; she was reserved and did not go out of her way to do anything outside of studying Pop and techniques in the genre.

"I would like that." Rachel smiled as she answered. The two new friends gave each other a quick hug and continued walking down the hall.

"Hey," Jessica said, "…you want to stop by an academy lab with me? I am meeting up with Lilly Chang. She has developed a new set of Beatlocks. She made them specifically for Sirens."

Lilly Chang did not have the best track record. Rachel began to contemplate the request. She did not want to reject her new friend's invitation, but she also did not want to get tangled with Lilly. There were rumors that Lilly had been caught using her powers to raise her rank inside the academy.

Due to Rachel's hesitation, Jessica added, "I know she has a bad rep, but trust me, she is not as bad as people make her out to be. I recently ran into her in the cafeteria and we started talking. She is very smart and we could learn from her. As you know, she is an expert and she told me she wouldn't mind teaching me more advanced moves if I ever wanted to learn."

Jessica made a good argument for Lilly; she didn't sound terrible.

"But what if she used her power on you? What if she is controlling you right now and you don't even know it?" Rachel asked.

"Oh, that's easy. Let me show you this trick. I started doing this when I learned about what Sirens could do. Whenever I am around Sirens with Beatlocks or experts like Lilly, I do this." Jessica raised her right hand. "I place my thumbnail into the tip of my middle finger. I press hard enough to leave an imprint." Jessica demonstrated with her right hand.

"But how would doing that let you know if you were controlled or not?" Rachel asked.

"They do not teach this in school, but I learned when someone is under the trance of a Siren, the first thing they do is drop their hands. This is a sign that the Siren has control. Then they do whatever the Siren tells them to do. No Siren would make them press their thumbnail into the tip of their middle finger. It's so random."

Relieved by this logic, Rachel agreed to go. "Ok, let's do it! Do you think she might agree to help me with advanced moves as well?"

"I don't see why not! Ever since those rumors started to spread, no one visits Lilly anymore. I am sure she is just happy to have people to talk to."

As they approached the lab, Jessica stopped Rachel. "Remember." Jessica raised her right hand. "Thumbnail to your fingertip." Rachel nodded, signaling that she remembered.

CONCEALED

Rachel and Jessica reached Lilly's lab. The doors were propped open. Jessica believed that Lilly did this intentionally in an attempt to seem trustworthy to her peers. This was only a theory; Jessica had not worked up enough courage to ask. Lilly's eyes lit up with joy when she saw Jessica walking into the lab. Jessica walked into a tight hug as Lilly shrieked in excitement.

"Oh Jess, thank you for stopping by!" She looked over at Rachel with a big smile as she released Jessica's hug.

"My name is Rachel, Mrs. Temptress. Very nice to meet you!"

"No need for the formalities, you can call me Lilly, dear. I am so glad the two of you stopped by! I just finished creating my new Beatlock prototype! You simply must give them a try." Lilly walked over to her desk in a fast-paced manner. She picked up what looked like hearing aids and looked back at the two girls. "OK, a quick history lesson. What happens in times of battle when someone sees a Siren equipped with Beatlocks?"

Rachel answered, "They activate A.N.C."

"Correct! Jessica, I see why the two of you are friends!"

Jessica looked at Rachel and the two girls smiled at each other as Lilly continued.

"They activate A.N.C. so they cannot be controlled by the Siren. There are three ways around that. You can create a device that amplifies sound at such a high volume that the A.N.C. becomes ineffective. That is pointless because the volume would have to be insanely loud just to get over the noise cancellation, not to mention it would have to be louder than the music playing over the Beatlocks as well. No, that is pointless. The second way is to find a way to hack into your opponent's Beatlocks. That process was eliminated when all the Beatlocks removed wireless technology. Can the two of you think of the third and final way?"

They thought to themselves. Jessica eventually spoke up. "Cooperation! Like at a concert. If people willingly let you use your powers, then there would be no need for any exploit."

"Yes, but in times of war no one would go to a concert. I do, however, see your implications. If I somehow portrayed myself as a different genre to gain an audience, I could see that working. Let's put a pin in that."

Rachel asked, "Why are we discussing war? We haven't been at war in years."

Lilly and Jessica looked over at Rachel, who appeared confused.

"Oh Rachel, we Sirens have been working nonstop trying to find an edge. You see, in the past our genre has used and exploited Pop to such an extent that no one trusts us. In return, we have lost our advantage. We have fallen from greatness and become vulnerable. Even though there is no war today, if we do not prepare for tomorrow's war, we will have already lost."

"I hope I am not being too direct, but it is so strange to hear concerns of trust coming from you."

Frustrated, Jessica called out, "Rachel." But she was stopped by Lilly.

"It's alright, Jessica, I love honesty." Lilly walked closer to Rachel. Rachel swallowed hard, slightly intimidated by Lilly but determined not to let her see it.

"I bet you've heard that I used my abilities to gain rank in the academy, am I right?"

Rachel looked over at Jessica, knowing she could not avoid such a direct question. Looking back at Lilly, she said, "Yes."

"I will tell you exactly what happened with that. It has direct connections to these." Once again, she showed off the hearing-aid devices.

"It was during a lecture. My professor was presenting his research to his bosses. For months before this lecture, I had been stressing to him that my discovery was exemplary and he should take a look at it, but he refused. I let him finish his presentation; however, they were not impressed. They confessed they expected more. Just before they walked out, I stopped them. I told them to stay and listen to what I had to say. Under normal circumstances, they would have just walked out. However, I was wearing these."

She held up the devices and finally revealed what they were. "These are a new set of Beatlocks, or as I would like to call them, the inner ears. I invented them personally. They are designed to rest at the entrance of your ear. Once both are in place, magnets pull the inner ears into your ear canal, completely hidden from sight. They are shaped in a way that surrounds your eardrum. The Siren is no longer a genre that can be ignored. People will not see us and immediately activate their A.N.C. That is exactly how I presented it to the faculty."

Jessica and Rachel were both impressed and scared. Did this mean that Lilly had the inner ears activated the whole time? Had she been controlling them?

"What happened next?" asked Rachel.

"Well, they loved it. Everyone at the academy loved the concept, the form factor, and the effectiveness. The problem lies in how I convinced the entire room to stay in the auditorium for the presentation. I only used the inner ears to stop them from walking out. My professor, fueled by envy, was convinced I was controlling them the whole time I presented my invention."

Rachel asked, "Why? After seeing your device work, what reservations did he have?"

"Well, because he refused to look at my project, I was unable to figure out how to fix the flaw in my initial prototypes." Lilly used her fingers to sweep her hair behind her ear, suggesting she was still wearing the inner ear device. "The only thing I wasn't able to finish testing was removing the inner ears."

"What happened to your professor?" Rachel asked.

"First, he was tasked with helping me design a new pair of inner ears and give users the ability to put them in and take them out. This was a task he could not take, admitting that a student had done something he couldn't. So, he refused. After a long debate, the academy decided that he was insubordinate. They fired him and assigned his lab to me. I tried to convince them otherwise, but they had made up their minds. Now here I am, with a tarnished reputation and an amazing invention I just want to share with the Singing Sirens."

After hearing the full story, Rachel felt terrible. She had judged Lilly before meeting her, which was a mistake. "I am so sorry for believing all of those terrible rumors. And I am sorry for questioning your loyalty to the Sirens."

Tearing up at Rachel's kind words, Lilly turned away and quickly dabbed her teary eye with her sleeve. "No need to apologize, Rachel, you are here, are you not?" Turning back to the two girls, Lilly continued. "Now, I have several inner ear devices ready to go. How would you two like to be the first to give them a test drive?"

Lilly reached out both of her arms, one toward Jessica and one toward Rachel. They both raised their arms and were presented with a pair of inner ears. Rachel stared at the small devices in her hand. Jessica, on the other hand, was already placing them into her ears.

"Woah, this is so cool. I can even hear better. It's like all sounds are amplified, but not too loud. How is it doing that?"

"Because of the first pair, which I wear. When I created them, I designed them to communicate all data with my computer. I have since programmed these new inner ears to detect which sounds are a priority and which sounds can be heard but are not loud."

Finally, Rachel built up the courage to ask, "How do you take these out? Have you fixed that issue?"

"I did fix that. Taking them out is simple. Tap three times on your inner ear and they will dismount your eardrum."

Jessica tapped three times and they popped out. She quickly looked at them and put them right back in. "I will probably never need to take these out again!"

Lilly let out a proud giggle. "Well, that was the plan — to create a device where a Siren could thrive without being viewed as a threat just for existing."

With reservations, Rachel asked, "Are you sure we can have these?"

"Yes, of course you can. I need more of you young people to wear them. Get used to them and let me know how it goes. If I get enough people to wear them, the university might allow me to make more. Who knows, maybe these could replace Beatlocks for all of the Singing Sirens! Just do not tell the other genres — that would defeat the purpose. And don't abuse your gifts."

Both Jessica and Rachel said, "Thank you." They all hugged and left the lab. "I can't believe she just gave us these inner ears."

When she thought about it, Rachel didn't know why Lilly gave them the inner ears either. "Maybe she just wants to test out the inner ears to prove that they work." Rachel still had not put them in her ears.

"Oh my goodness, Rachel, what are you doing tonight?"

"I was planning on practicing charm infusion."

"Isn't that when you infuse objects with charm? That's an intermediate move. You're already studying to advance?"

"No time like the present!"

"You're not wrong. How about we do that together, but tomorrow? Tonight, you should go with me to the theater. There is a documentary about dubstep playing."

Knowledge of other genres has proven valuable to everyone. Research suggests that if people can understand what each person draws from their genre of music, then the user could manipulate their genre with a more potent result.

"That sounds good to me. I have not seen anything on dubstep yet and it sounds really interesting."

"Yay! Ok, I'm going home to change. Let's meet up at the theater?"

"Ok, yeah, I'll see you there!"

As they were leaving, Rachel remembered the finger trick. She looked at her hand. There was a thumbnail print, but it was faint. She couldn't remember when she stopped putting pressure on it. Was it when she was handed the inner ears? Or was she placed in a trance? Then she thought about Lilly's story. Rachel wondered if she was overreacting. She put the inner ears into her pocket and decided not to let it bother her. Lilly seemed misunderstood and not the evil person everyone had painted her to be. However, the thought still lingered in her mind.

Escape

Rachel arrived at the theater a little earlier than planned. She wanted to be able to get some snacks before the lines got super long. As she arrived at the concession stand, she was surprised to see Jessica already in line. Rachel was happy at the thought that she and Jessica were more alike than she realized.

"Hey Jess, I didn't expect to see you here so early."

Jessica was equally surprised. "Maestro!" The two girls embraced, and Jessica continued, "I like to come early for movies like this. It's the only way to make sure you get a good seat."

Rachel ordered an iced water and chicken strips while Jessica ordered popcorn and water. "How dare you come to the movies and not get a popcorn?"

"I like the taste of popcorn, but I can't stand the way the kernels get stuck in my teeth. I wouldn't be able to enjoy the movie," answered Rachel.

Jessica responded, "Yeah, that does happen from time to time. If you ever change your mind, you can share with me."

"Thanks, Jess. So, tell me about your seating choices. Do you like to sit closer to the front or the back of the movie?"

"I like to sit right in the middle. If I get too close, I can't see the full screen. When I am in the back, I don't feel fully immersed. The middle is the best, hands down."

"Glad I'm going with such an expert. I come early to avoid the snack line, but I don't put too much thought into where I sit."

"Then you're in for a treat, come on!"

The two girls made their way to the theater entrance. They began to register their names for the assigned seats when Jessica discovered her favorite seats were already taken. Seating in the auditorium was nearly wide open; however, the best spots had already been reserved. The seats Jessica picked were second best from her perspective. They were directly in the middle of the screen from left to right. They were nearly in the center from front to back, but it was not perfect. There was a group of people that stole the best seats, one row in front of them.

"I can't believe they got our seats," cried out Jessica.

Rachel let out a little laugh. "It's ok, Jess, it's just one row different. I'm sure it will still be a great show."

"Yeah, but I promised you the best show."

"Don't worry. Next time we will come two hours early and get that spot, that will show 'em!" Just then, they noticed a rather cute boy waving to them. They had no idea who this boy was but were flattered that he was waving at them.

Both girls giggled as they ducked down into the crowd and ran to their seats. "Jess, are you still wearing those inner ears?"

"Yeah, I am, isn't it amazing! The audio is just perfect. I'm so confused about how they take in all the noises from this theater and lower the volume to a whisper, while I can hear you perfectly. What do you think?"

"I uh… I still have not put them in yet."

"What, why not?"

"I don't know. I mean, Lilly seems super nice, but I'm not sure I fully trust her. She had those inner ears in the whole time, did you know that when you met her?"

"Well no, she never told me that, but that is the point of the devices, right? To make sure that no one knows you're wearing them. If she told every Siren she met, they would just say worse things about her."

"You are right about that. But what about the finger trick? Did you check your finger to see if you had the nail print?"

Jessica took a moment to think before she responded, "No, I actually forgot to check. I got pretty excited about getting the inner ears, I didn't even look. I ran home and convinced my brother to do my chores."

With that confession, Jessica put both hands up to her mouth as if to seal her lips.

Laughing, Rachel jokingly confronted her. "Jess! You are not supposed to use your powers on your brother!"

They both laughed some more before Jessica replied, "I just wanted to make sure they worked, haha. I won't use my powers on him again, I promise."

As the two continued laughing, the lights in the theater began to dim. The show was beginning. The music started and the room erupted with excitement. Rachel had never seen such a live performance. The light show was so enchanting as it paired perfectly with the music.

Without warning, it was brought to an abrupt end. The room went dark and a strange, masked figure appeared on the screen. The person on the screen began to speak. "Good evening, Bass Masters. We must perform an auditory test of the theater speakers. This will only take a minute." The speakers in the theater began to play random music.

"This is something they should have done long before the show," said Jessica.

"What?" Rachel could not hear very well. The music playing over the speakers was very loud. On top of that, they were playing music she had never heard before, which confused her senses. She felt a wave of emotion come over her as she heard the sound of jazz music fill the auditorium. The feeling was slightly familiar, but different. Almost instantly, her seat was illuminated.

A strange man wearing the same outfit as the person on the screen then approached Rachel and said, "I need you to come with me." Rachel grabbed Jessica's hand, but the man stopped her and said, "No, she will stay, you will be back soon." Rachel began to protest; however, as she looked around the auditorium, she noticed she was not the only person selected. There were other people following these strangers out of the theater. Rachel instantly pressed her thumbnail into the tip of her middle finger and made sure she was not being manipulated.

Rachel began to walk reluctantly with the strange man toward the exit of the auditorium. Before exiting, she gave one last glance at where she and Jessica were seated. Then she noticed that Jessica was trying to signal something. With both of her hands raised to her ears, she was tapping them. Rachel realized Jessica was telling her to put in the inner ears.

As Rachel walked out of the auditorium, the hairs on the back of her neck began to rise when she was no longer en route to the lobby. Where were they taking her, and what did she have in common with all the other people being escorted out? Rachel was perplexed. She still didn't trust Lilly enough to wear the inner ears, but she also did not feel comfortable with the situation she was currently in. Against her best judgment, Rachel put in the inner ears quickly before anyone noticed her. After all, the point of the inner ears was to be discreet and unnoticed.

Rachel was put into a group of four others. She did not recognize any of the people in the group, so she remained quiet as she was still trying to get used to having the inner ears in. The sound was just as amazing as Jessica described. She could hear everything and nothing at the same time. Whatever she focused on, the sound was crystal clear and everything else got quiet. Her group was led out of the theater through the rear exit.

Rachel decided to put the inner ears to the test. She took a look around. There were five black SUVs parked just outside the theater. The SUV closest to her group had all the doors open and she could see two strange men standing near each other. They appeared to be talking. Rachel focused on them. Like magic, all the nearby sounds were quieted and she could hear the two men talking as if she was right next to them. "Get this last group loaded up so we can get out of here."

Shocked, Rachel stood there frozen in fear of what was going on. Why was this happening, where would they be taken? Just then, one of the two strangers she heard talking approached her group. "All right everyone, I need to make sure you don't have any weapons or Beatlocks. Line up so I can frisk you."

The first person frisked was a nice-looking kid. He appeared to be about fifteen years old, maybe a beginner. He did not have any weapons or Beatlocks. The second person was a girl who looked as though she was around the same age as Rachel, maybe seventeen years old. The stranger found a set of Beatlocks on her and began to confiscate them. She attempted to refuse, but the man insisted she would get them back after she was properly identified. The lady allowed the man to take her Beatlocks.

The third person in Rachel's group was frisked. He had a consword and a pair of Beatlocks. Rachel remembered conswords were weapons used by people who practiced the country genre. He did not put up a fight. He allowed his belongings to be taken by the stranger.

The fourth person was another girl. As the man approached her, she quickly tried to put on her Beatlocks. The man grabbed her and they both struggled for control. A second stranger came and kicked the girl's feet from under her. The girl fell to the ground, which gave the stranger leverage to pry the Beatlocks out of her hands. The group protested with the guards, complaining that they did not have to be so physical with her.

The group was yelled at to calm down. "If you guys don't cooperate, we will use force! Just do as we say, and no one will get hurt." That man then walked back up to the front of the car as if he were the driver.

Rachel was then approached and frisked by the assaultive stranger. Her heart began to thump out of her chest and she was worried the stranger would see the inner ears. But it worked; she was able to keep the inner ears without being noticed. Everyone was ushered into the SUV besides the girl who was still on the ground. Rachel offered her hand to the girl as she walked past, but the stranger smacked it away. "She doesn't need any help. Right, Ava?"

The stranger raised his foot back as if he were preparing to kick this girl. Was her name Ava? How did he know her name? Did he know Rachel and the others? Rachel's mind raced a million miles a second as this stranger's foot was loaded back, preparing to kick this helpless girl lying on the ground.

Rachel decided to take control of the situation and began to sing. "Stop!" The man who was preparing to kick Ava instantly froze. His hands dropped to his sides and he faced Rachel. The whole group of people watched Rachel as she used her powers without Beatlocks. Rachel continued. "Give Ava her Beatlocks and listen to me, you. Give the Beatlocks back that you took from the other two." Rachel, not prepared for this impromptu freestyle, was relieved to see it was working. The man took the confiscated Beatlocks off his belt and handed them to Ava, as well as the other girl and boy.

Rachel exited the SUV and motioned for everyone else to exit. She didn't want to speak to them for fear they might believe she put them in a trance as well. When the country boy exited the SUV, he also took his consword back from the man. The girl and boy both equipped their Beatlocks and stood behind Rachel. Ava slowly stood up behind Rachel and equipped her Beatlocks.

While still in control, Rachel continued. "Now take off your Beatlocks and put them down. Repeatedly raise your foot and smash them into the ground." With the rhyming phrase, the stranger took off his Beatlocks and continuously stomped on them, breaking them completely and forcing them into the ground.

Rachel, with her eyes still locked on the stranger, thought to herself, "What next?" She didn't have to think long before the second stranger came walking toward the back of the SUV.

"What's taking so long?" The stranger stopped as he could see the group of kids, armed with Beatlocks.

"Uh, help," Rachel called upon her new friend. The stranger quickly equipped his A.N.C., and the fight was on.

Out of anger and pain, Ava began to use her vibrations, which caused the stranger stomping his Beatlocks into the ground to fall. Still in a trance, he continued to stomp and kick at his headset as he struggled to maintain stability.

The country boy quickly closed the distance between him and the stranger still on his feet. He began swinging the consword at him; however, his opponent was skilled and appeared to easily dodge the kid's attacks.

The little boy ran toward the SUV and appeared to be looking for something. The SUV was about to tip from Ava's vibrations. Rachel looked over at Ava and pointed out the boy in the SUV. Ava stopped her vibrations. The boy appeared to have found another pair of Beatlocks and put them on. He then retreated toward Rachel.

The boy watched as the country kid and the stranger fought. The boy said, "There!" All of a sudden, the stranger's feet snapped together. It appeared as though he could not move them. This gave the country kid the upper hand. The smaller boy must have metal abilities, as the stranger had steel-toe boots. The country boy quickly advanced on the stranger in a zigzag fashion before he struck him with the handle of his consword, incapacitating the stranger.

All the kids grouped back up. The little boy then raised his hands toward the SUV they had been in. In no time, the SUV began to rise off the ground. The SUV was flipped upside down and slammed back down.

"We need to get out of here," suggested Rachel.

The unknown girl asked, "Do you guys see that staircase over there?" Rachel and the group looked to their right. There was a staircase that led down into the subway.

"We see it," said the country boy.

The unknown girl continued her instructions, "When I tell you, close your eyes and run toward the staircase. Keep going until you are all the way into the subway. You must keep your eyes closed, ok?"

Rachel said, "Got it! What are you going to do?"

"I'm going to light it up! Now go!"

RECON

The group all took one last look at the staircase before they closed their eyes and ran. As they ran, the last girl finally utilized her abilities. This girl was powered by gospel music and could control light. She let out the most intense and bright explosion of light, temporarily blinding anyone who was looking in her direction. She then ran to catch up with her group.

As she reached them, she reminded them to keep their eyes closed until they reached the bottom of the stairs and out of the range of her divine illumination.

After escaping the threat of combat, the group was able to take a deep breath and let their guard down. Ava took off her Beatlocks. The rest of the group followed suit in a show of confidence. Reminded by the removal of Beatlocks, the group looked at Rachel, who appeared to have used her abilities without them.

Ava asked, "How were you able to use your abilities without Beatlocks?"

"Oh, I didn't." Rachel took out the inner ears and showed them to the group. "A professor of mine designed them. They fully surround my eardrum. It is a bit of an improvement over A.N.C."

The country boy spoke up. "So you're a Siren with Beatlocks that we can't see? We never know if you're equipped or not? Great."

"Hey, she did just save us back there," Ava interjected. "She had every opportunity to use her abilities to abandon us. She could have even made us forget she was ever there. But she decided to save us all. Give her some respect."

The country boy thought about that for a second before he admitted, "You're right, Ava, I'm sorry. My name is Wyatt."

"It's ok, nice to meet you. My name is Rachel. What are your names?"

The little boy stepped up. "I'm Riley."

"My name is Grace, Grace Carter."

Rachel asked the group, "Do any of you know what was going on?"

No answers came from the group. "I did notice something," Ava said. "But maybe it is nothing."

Grace encouraged Ava to speak up. "No, go ahead, what is it?"

"Well, when they were 'testing the music,' that was when I noticed the seats started to illuminate. At first, I thought we were selected based on the music. But my seat illuminated during what sounded like rap music. I am empowered by dubstep. Why would I be selected with hip hop?"

The group unanimously agreed that they were incorrectly identified. Rachel was Pop but selected during jazz, Wyatt was Country but selected during rock, Riley was Metal but selected during chopped and screwed, and Grace was Christian but selected with soul music.

"Ok, so the pattern isn't that we were selected with our empowering genre," Grace thought out loud.

Riley seemed to pick up where Grace left off. "The pattern is that we were paired with a genre that does not give us power. Do you think it is our weakness?"

Concerned, Wyatt added, "I did feel strange right before my seat lit up."

Grace agreed. "So did I."

"The feeling I got wasn't weakness. I felt strong," said Ava.

Rachel agreed. "It almost felt like the feeling I get when I use my Pop powers. But different. I don't know how to explain it."

"Ava!"

The group all looked up toward the staircase.

"Oscar... That's my brother."

Ava started to run toward the stairs before she was stopped by Rachel and Grace. "Ava, wait," pleaded Rachel.

"If you go back out there, they could find us," added Grace. "They already know who we are. If we go back to our families, we might put them in danger."

With eyes filled with tears, Riley asked, "We can't go home?"

"Not until we find out who those strangers were and where they went with the rest of the people they kidnapped. My sister was in one of those other SUVs. I have to find her."

"How are we supposed to find them?" asked Wyatt.

"We work together," said Ava, deciding not to respond to Oscar. With great sadness in her voice, she continued, "We all have abilities that could help us find the others if we work together."

Rachel nodded in agreement. "That's right. Wyatt, your abilities are centered around nature and the environment, right? Maybe you could try to use your powers to track the SUVs?"

"I will definitely give it a shot!"

"Perfect, then that is the plan. Ava, can you tell how far this tunnel goes?"

Ava put her Beatlocks back on and put her hand to the ground. She was able to sense the minute but constant vibrations in the subway. After a moment or two, Ava took off the Beatlocks and said, "It seems like the next exit is about two blocks away."

"Ok, let's take the tunnel, just in case those guys are still lurking around."

Riley spoke up, "But I was told to never walk on the tracks."

"It's ok, Riley," said Wyatt. "We will be quick and I will make sure nothing happens to you, my man." It was clear that Wyatt had charm even without being powered by country music. Riley perked up and grabbed Wyatt's extended hand.

They all hopped down onto the subway tracks and began jogging to the next stop. After making it to the exit, they slowly walked up the stairs, hoping that the strangers did not track them through the tunnels.

Wyatt took a look around. They were still very much in an urban environment. "Well, I was hoping for a little more nature, but we have only gone two blocks. There is too much noise for me to communicate with the environment. Sorry, guys."

Rachel began to think. In the group, they had someone who could control vibrations, light, metal, the environment, and people. Then she came up with another idea. "Grace, you said your sister was taken as well, yeah?"

"Yes, we were taken at the same time but split into different groups."

"Can't you two sense each other or something?"

"Yeah, you are thinking of our guiding beacon, but she would need a pair of Beatlocks. I know hers were taken before she was forced inside another SUV."

"Have you ever tried it with only one of you wearing the Beatlocks?"

"No, I haven't tried, but I am pretty sure she would need them to emit a sort of beacon for me to follow."

"What if the Beatlocks only amplify her beacon? You two are sisters. I am sure you know her better than anyone else. I am certain you can find your sister, Grace. Give it a shot."

Knowing it could not hurt to try, Grace agreed. Grace put on the Beatlocks and began to focus. A thin stream of light shot into the sky. The stream of light seemed to collect above and formed the shape of a sphere. The group watched and held their breath, waiting for some kind of indication that it was working. All of a sudden, the beam of light shot back down to Grace.

Assuming it had not worked, Rachel approached Grace. "Thanks for trying. It is alright. We will think of something."

"No," Grace said. "I know where they are."

The group traveled a few miles out of the city on foot. They appeared to grow closer as they talked to each other the entire time. They talked about their abilities, what they had learned, what their goals were, and all the things they wished to accomplish. It seemed as though every one of them was ambitious and very talented, another trait Rachel noticed they all had in common.

Rachel had still been thinking about why they were taken. She knew they were all selected for a genre of music not specific to them. They all felt a surge of power while the music was playing. They were all natural learners in their respective fields. What could all of this mean?

Rachel's thoughts were cut short as Grace said, "That's it." She pointed down the street. "That's where my sister is."

They approached a rather large, one story building. There was a large bay door in front and it appeared to have tire tracks that led inside. The group ducked out of sight, just in case anyone was keeping surveillance on the place. "Ava, can you use your vibrations again to tell us what is going on inside the building?"

"On it." Ava used her abilities again. This time, while she had one hand on the ground, she used her other hand to draw a map in the dirt of what she was seeing. The group watched as she drew what appeared to be the exterior of the building. In the middle of the building, she placed a group of circles. There were three points of entry and there was a dot inside each one.

Ava stood up and explained her drawing. "It appears that all the people who were kidnapped were sitting in the middle of the room with a few strangers pacing around them. There are three possible entrances, but they are guarded. It is strange though. I could sense the emotion of the group. None of them appeared to be scared. It was like they were all calm, relaxed even. Rachel, do you think you could convince one of the guards to let us in?"

"I don't think so. I need to make sure we are face to face. If I try to convince someone through a wall, I could compromise our position."

"Ava!"

That was it. The group had been caught. They were so close, but they were not fast enough. The group turned to see who would seal their fate.

"Oscar!"

"Jessica!"

"Rachel!"

The rest of the group was confused. They watched as Oscar and Ava embraced. Jessica and Rachel gave each other the tightest hug either of them had ever had.

"How did you find us?" Ava asked.

"Elijah and I were, well, we tracked your vibrations in this direction. He could not come with me, but as I was making my way here, I ran into Jessica." Oscar was relieved he did not accidentally tell everyone about the device he and Elijah had been working on.

"I spoke with Professor Lilly. As it turns out, she had a hunch that you guys might have been taken here."

Confused, Rachel gave Jessica a look. Then she realized she was talking about the inner ears.

"She had a tracker in the inner ears?"

"Rachel!" From the lack of expression on the faces in the group, Jessica realized they already knew about them. "You told them?"

"I had no choice. We were being kidnapped and I had to fight back. But do not worry, I trust them. They will not say anything."

Wyatt, with his Beatlocks equipped, utilized his heartfelt communication. "Guys, let's discuss this later. We were right in the middle of figuring out how to rescue the others. If we all work together like earlier, I know we can save them all." His voice had a direct impact on the group. He renewed their team spirit and got them ready to fight.

Rachel, aware of all the powers in the group, had a plan put together. With pure determination in her voice, she addressed the group and spoke. "All right, guys, we have one chance to get this right. Listen closely."

STRESSED

"Welcome to the show! How many seats would you like" asked the excited employee of the theatre.

"I only need the one." Said Max, "None of my friends could make it today."

"That's ok, sometimes, being alone enhances your ability to enjoy the show. No distractions means you get to see and hear everything in front of you." The skilled staff member furthered Max's decision to still attend the show alone.

With a smile on her face, the employee with the name tag of "Tracy" handed Max his ticket stub. "Thank you Tracy. I wasn't sure if I should go alone or not, but now I feel a lot better."

"My pleasure. enjoy the show!"

With a new level of excitement, Max walked into the theater ready to fully ingest the show. As he walked in, he saw a class mate of his, Riley walking in with his family.

Max watched him for a while, waiting for the opportunity to waive. As time went on, Max figured he should stop watching as his glance was transitioning into a stare. Just as he began to look away, Riley looked in his direction.

Max quickly turned back to Riley and started to waive, but the moment was over and Riley was no longer looking. This waive did not go to waste as two girls walking in assumed the waive was for them. The two girls looked at each other and giggled. Before they ducked into the crowd and disappeared. Completely embarrassed, Max decided to just walk to his seat before he unintentionally made any new friends.

Max walked to his seat with his head down. He counted down the letters in his head as he walked, "A. B. C. D. E. F. G. H." Nothing embarrassing happened. So he continued looking down and started to count the numbers to his seat. "1. 2. 3. 4. 5." Finally, he reached his seat. He noticed that no one was sitting around him and became a little excited at the thought. Maybe he would get lucky and have no one next to him. Max believed it was always a treat when there was an empty seat next to him. He didn't have to think about elbow space, did not have to share snacks, and wouldn't be distracted by someone who couldn't stay off their phone.

Max sat down, still optimistic and excited for the show to start. Max looked down at his watch, there was only two minutes left until the show began. Max pulled out his beat-locks and examined them. He recently moved on from the beginners level and became an intermediate user of Metal. The evaluators at his performance said he was electrifying. Another said it strikingly perfect. And so he became, Thunderstrike

Max was still impressed with himself. Originally, Max's dream was to become the worlds greatest drummer. He planned to achieve this by continuous refinement of drumming techniques, exploring various styles, and pushing boundaries of rythmic innovation. One night, during a performance, he obtained a strange feeling. Max looked around the building, and he could see all the metal. It looked as if it was all behind highlighted. He could see the steel beams through the walls. At first, he had no idea what was going on. After the show, he talked to his band mates who suggested he was a Metal Titan and Max's life has never been the same.

Now Max has been practicing the intermediate moves with intentions on promoting to expert as soon as possible. Max believes that if he can master all 10 abilities, he could then achieve his goal of being the best drummer in the Titans.

The lights began to dim which created a roar over the crowd. Everyone began to cheer in excitement as the music started to play. The sound amplified by the strategically timed light show playing in sync with the fast paced beat of dub-step music. Everything was brought to a stop in a split second. The music and lights cut off, and a stranger in a mask appeared on screen.

"Good evening, Bass Masters. We must perform an auditory test of the theater speakers. This will only take a minute." An eerie feeling came over Max. Everyone around him began complaining about the inconvenience which made him feel especially alone. Music began playing over the speakers.

The music continuously changed genres. Prior to the change, Max noticed there were a select few seats around the theatre that illuminated. The people in those seats were being escorted out of the theatre. Max's seat lit up and a stranger approached him. The masked man, equipped with beat-locks said, "Come with me."

"I'm not going anywhere" said max.

"This isn't a request. Just cooperate and you will return to your seat shortly."

Max prepared to argue when the music changed again, he noticed that one of the two girls he accidentally waived at were selected. She began to walk with the stranger. Unconsciously, Max was hoping to meet her so he agreed to go. He was able to convince himself, "If she's going with them, then this can't be anything bad."

Max was escorted out of the Auditorium. While walking with the stranger, he was placed in to a group of four other people whom he'd never met before. In front of his group, there was another group of five. Behind him, there was another group of five. That group included the girl he wanted to meet and his classmate Riley. The group was led out of the theater through the rear emergency exit. The group ahead of Max had been searched and all beat-locks were taken.

"Stand in a line, I will take any weapons and beat-locks you may have. Everything will be returned to you as soon as we confirm your identities."

Max thought to himself. It had been strongly suggested not to bring beat-locks or weapons into the theatre after the last fight a group had, but it wasn't against the law. Maybe they were cracking down on it. They most likely were documenting who brought what and why. There was no way he would be arrested for this, would he? The time came when Max was to be searched. To make things easy, Max reached into his pocket and pulled out his beat-locks. The stranger quickly raised his right hand towards his personal pair beat-locks as if he was going to engage the Absolute Noise Cancellation, also known as ANC.

Max quickly offered up his beat-locks, as a show of faith. The stranger, seemingly relieved, lowered his right hand,

and grabbed Max's beat-locks with his left. "Thank you" said the Stranger.

Max was ushered into the back seat of an all black SUV with the rest of his group. There was one Stranger in the front seat who started to speak on a potable radio. "Unit 2, secured and ready for transport." The second stranger, who collected all the beat-locks, sat in the rear seat of the SUV facing forward.

Max could see the last group being searched through the rear window. The calmed demeanor faded from his face when he saw a female struggling with one of the strangers.

The stranger in the backseat of the SUV noticed this shift in Max's disposition and looked out the back window. A second stranger assisted the first who was struggling with the girl and kicked her feet from under her. The strangers snatched the beat-locks and continued loading the third SVU.

The stranger sitting with Max returned looking forward while shaking his head. "There is always one. And I thought it was going to be you." Max, looked down at his feet. He began thinking this was not normal. This was not ok. Max felt his body shaking with fear and anger. Should he try and help the girl? There was no way. He had no weapon and did not have a pair of beat-locks.

Max began to shake more intensely with rage. He was visibly shaking. It didn't take Max long to realize that he wasn't actually shaking, he was being shook. Someone was using vibrational powers. A Bass Master? Max looked back up and out the window to see a masked stranger stomping out what appeared to be his personal set of beat-locks.

That was more consistent with a Singing Siren as Max knew the stranger would not do that intentionally. The growing power of the vibration validated the presence of a Bass Master. The stranger sitting with Max did not appear to notice the vibrations or did not care. The stranger then spoke, "It will only increase your fear if you watch. Just stay calm, and nothing will happen to you."

The stranger did feel the vibrations. He must just be so confident in his squad that he was convinced they were the ones causing the scene. "Hey," called the backseat stranger to the front seat, "tell unit 3 to hurry this up, we don't have all day."

"Unit 3. Enough with the show of force, lets hit the road."

Max could see a stranger from the third SUV grab the radio and say "Copy." The stranger exited the front seat and started walking towards the back of the SUV. When the stranger saw all of the passengers outside of the SUV, now all equipped with beat-locks, he activated his ANC and engaged one of them. One of the passengers started swinging at the stranger with a sword that Max had never seen before. The stranger was insanely quick and able to dodge each swing of the sword.

The stranger sitting with Max started to look back and find out what was taking so long. It appeared the kids might be able to take this last stranger out, but if two additional strangers jumped into the fight, they just might not make it out alive!

Just before the stranger turned all the way around, Max called out, "Where are we going!?" This caught the strangers attention and delayed his gaze from looking at the third SUV.

"We will explain once you get there. If I tell you now, you will have more questions. I do not plan on repeating the same thing to each of you. Better if I say it once and answer questions all at once."

The stranger started to look back again so Max quickly spoke up. "What if I don't want to go!?"

This again delayed the inevitable and Max achieved eye contact with the stranger. "With what is happening out there, you think you have a choice?"
The stranger then looked back. This time, Max had nothing to say. He was fueled with fear at what the stranger just told him. It became clear now, he didn't have a choice.

They were all in trouble. they had committed some crime and this was serious. Were the people revolting outside more seasoned criminals? Maybe the stranger should know what was going on.

When the stranger finally looked back, he saw one guard laid out and another obviously under a trance as he was repeatedly stomping the minuscule resemblance of beat-locks. The stranger yelled up to the front seat, "Unit 3 has a breach!"

The stranger in the front seat looked through the rearview mirror and could only see the kids they grouped up and began running away. There was one kid still standing. It was a girl and she began to glow. The stranger knew this was a display of gospel music.

The stranger in the back seat opened the back door as if he were going after the kids.

"Close the door!" Yelled the stranger in the driver's seat. Without hesitation, the stranger in the backseat slammed the door shut. "Unit 1, Unit 3 was compromised, engage the divinity shields!"

All of a sudden, all of the windows turned pure black. Max was unable to see anything outside. The front windshield lit up with a full heads-up display. This gave a full augmented visualization of the road ahead of them. The driver of the first SUV began to drive off and Max's SUV quickly followed suit.

Max could tell there was a bright flash outside. The once black windows illuminated into a light gray color as if it were fighting off a mass amount of light. This lasted for approximately ten seconds before everything went black again. As soon as the windows went black, the driver returned the windows to normal and spun the car around to face the abandoned and destroyed SVU.

"Should we go after them" asked the back seat stranger. "No, we will get them later. Let's move forward as planned." The driver quickly spun back around and caught up to the first SUV.

Max had no idea what was going on or what was going to happen. All he knew for sure was that he was out classed and unarmed. If he wanted to survive the night, he would have to cooperate and hope for the best. There was no other choice. One thought lingered on his mind. Were the others ok? Will he ever see Riley or that girl again?

DUALIST

It had to be about a twenty-minute drive before they arrived. They were quickly ushered out of the SUVs, and Max did not have time to look around and get an idea of where they were. Once inside, Max came to the conclusion they were in some sort of training center. It was a wide-open layout with several sections designed for different genres. Max was surprised to see that so many different genres were working together. The idea of punishment left his mind as there did not appear to be any jail cells or prisoners.

They all walked to the center of the room where there were chairs waiting for them. One of the strangers gathered five chairs and took them away from the group. Those chairs must have been for the kids that escaped earlier. Finally left alone, the group of ten began to chatter.

One of the kids broke the silence and asked, "What do you guys think is going on?"

Another answered, "I have no idea, but I am about to freak if they don't explain soon."

A third asked, "Did you guys see what happened to the third SUV?"

Max responded, "They rebelled. They fought the two strangers and escaped. One of them was glowing before the strangers turned all the windows black."

A fourth jumped in, "Then there was a large flash?"

Max continued, "Right! Once the flash was gone, the windows returned to normal and the kids were gone."

"That flash was my sister Grace! I know it. She was in the last SUV, and we are Luminescent Believers. Are you all LBs?"

Max answered, "No, I'm a Metal Titan. How about we all introduce ourselves? Maybe we will learn something about why we were singled out. My name is Max, and like I said, I am a Metal Titan."

"I am Tanya Carter, an LB."

"I am Jasmine Turner, I'm a Time Twister."

"Owen Harris, Rustic Guardian."

"Maya Turner, Jasmine's cousin, and a Bass Master."

"Malik Jackson, Lyrical Windweaver."

"Emma Stone, Empathetic Harmonizer."

"My name is Jamie Brown, AKA Rhythm Ruler. I am a Singing Siren."

"I'm Casey Reed, Rocking Resilience."

"Olivia Carter. I am cousins with Tanya and Grace, but I am a Sentimental Savant."

There was a bit of silence now that they had all been introduced. Everyone couldn't help but think to themselves.

"We are all different genres. Did anyone else put that together?"

"That's exactly what I was thinking," said Tanya.

Emma asked, "Do you think they were trying to get one of each genre?"

"I don't think that was the goal," answered Tanya. "I am an LB; however, I was picked while rock music was playing. Clearly, I'm not a part of the Rocking Resilience." Tanya turned toward Casey. "No offense."

"None taken," Casey responded. "You don't seem to have an ounce of resilience in you."

"I really did not mean any disrespect, Casey. I just meant I already stated I was a Luminescent Believer, and I can't be both."

"That's it!" interrupted Owen. "I was also picked during an alternate genre. I'm assuming this is the same for everyone?"

There was a resounding yes from the entire group as they all nodded their heads.

"Do you think there was some kind of mistake?" asked Jamie. "Clearly we cannot be two different genres, right?"

Emma spoke up, "I do remember reading a book about someone who was powered by two genres. I think they considered themselves a hybrid genre or an infused genre or something like that. I thought it was fiction, though. I didn't think anyone could actually wield two genres at once."

"That's impossible," burst out Casey. "I'm in the dark about what is going on just like the rest of you, but don't let your minds wander. Has anyone met anyone who is empowered by two genres?"

No one in the group answered.

"Exactly." Casey finished as she crossed her arms.

Tanya began again. "Come to think of it, I stopped looking for my muse as soon as I became empowered by gospel music. Same with my sister."

"Why continue looking once you gained your powers?" added Max.

"No, she's right," Maya added. "I bet everyone stops testing different genres once they develop powers for one genre. What if we really could be powered by two types?"

"I am not saying I agree," Malik joined in, "but if it is possible, what would that sound like? Would the music be composed together? Would the user switch genres mid-battle?"

Max began to speak, "The advantages…" before they heard the loud slam of the door. The group looked back to see two additional strangers joining the ranks.

"Great, more of them," said Emma.

"No," Max suggested. "Those were the two who were in charge of the third SUV. I wonder if they caught the others who got away."

Tanya stated, "I would assume not since they are empty-handed and the others seem pretty upset."

The strangers sent the two back outside while the other four started walking back toward the group. One appeared to be the leader. He walked with a sense of grace about him, a certain display of confidence. He walked to the front of the group while the others mingled in the back of the room.

"It is about time I inform you why you are all here."

Max interrupted, "What happened to the others!?"

The stranger let silence fill the air as he stared in Max's direction. He slowly reached up and took off his mask, followed by his Beatlocks. The man appeared normal, not someone they would expect to be lurking around in a mask and snatching kids out of a theater.

"The 'others' you speak of refused to comply and assaulted two of our members."

"That's not true!" Max insisted. "I watched those two assault a girl, which caused the others to defend her. If they never assaulted her, that whole situation could have been avoided."

"Max, the incompetence of those two will be addressed, I assure you." Max fell silent at the realization that the stranger knew him by name. What else did he know?

"As I was saying," the stranger continued, "it is time I inform you why you are all here. For generations now, genres have divided us. That was not always the case. When mankind discovered that they could be powered by music, we all worked together to create a peaceful world. It wasn't until the other genres realized that the Singing Sirens were using their powers to control the masses and shape the world in their image. This caused the world's first Battle of the Bands."

This was all common knowledge. No one in the group was surprised at this information. If anything, they were confused about why they were getting this history lesson.

"This war shattered the world into shards of what it used to be. Genres separated and remained that way while Singing Sirens were outcast by everyone."

While it was widely known, it did not lighten the blow for Jamie. She swallowed hard at hearing this information and looked down at her feet.

"That is nothing to be ashamed of, Jamie." She looked back up at the stranger. "Our ancestors do not dictate our characters of today." A small grin fought its way to the surface of her face as she was not normally complimented in such a way.

"After defeating the Sirens of old, and the war was over, nothing was the same. The world did not go back to the way it was before. Genres stayed separate and all have been looking for ways to gain control of the others. My group has been collecting information on each genre, and we believe that a war is inevitable. This information has forced us into a decision. Do we sit back and see the way things play out, or do we take action and try to minimize the casualties? We have decided to take action and stop this war before it happens, at all costs."

"And how do you plan to do that?" asked Max.

"All in due time, young Titan. For now, I wish to invite you into our ranks as new recruits. This has been done at a much smaller scale throughout the generations."

"How is that?" asked Emma. "I have never heard anything like this before."

"And that is done with intention, Emma. You see, long ago, a group of us discovered that we had the unique ability to utilize two different types of genres."

The group was shocked to hear what was just said. They all looked around at each other, confirming they all just heard the same thing.

"That's right. This type of music is considered a hybrid genre as it consists of any combination of two genres. When a person is powered by a hybrid genre, they are considered a Dualist, which is what we call our group.

Dualists consist of two sub-categories. This group is powered by two different genres mashed together to create a new sound."

"Oh come on!" Malik rudely interrupted. "Imagine two genres 'mashed' together, that would sound terrible."

"Malik, I understand this can be confusing. Let me give you an example. You are a Lyrical Windweaver, powered by hip hop, correct?"

"That's right," Malik answered.

"Well, did you know that hip hop was not the original genre?"

"That's right!" Tanya answered. "Hip hop was the combination of disco and funk."

"Correct, Tanya."

Confused, Tanya asked, "Well, what happened to disco and funk? I've never heard of anyone powered by either."

"The answer is simple. The composers and users were all killed in the Battle of the Bands. This is exactly why the Dualists intend to prevent a second war from happening."

Max spoke up, "You said there was a second category of Dualists?"

"Yes, Max. The other type of Dualist is someone who has the ability to master both genres independently. There are rumors that some had the ability to harness both types, but there are none within our ranks."

"You said that you have recruited in the past. How is it possible we have never heard of you?"

"Once you agree to be a part of the Dualists, you must return to your lives and never tell anyone about your initiation. Not your friends, not your family, no one. You will return here to practice your craft and become an elite."

Casey finally chimed in, "Those two from Unit 3 did not seem so 'elite' if you ask me. They were taken down by a group who thought they were only powered by one genre."

"As embarrassing as this is, that was never meant to happen. We usually do not recruit in such large numbers; however, we are pressed for time. We have come to learn that the Sirens have developed a device that could bring them back into the seat of power."

Once again, Jasmine dropped her head.

"That is where you come in, Jasmine."

Encouraged, she looked back up.

"Our goal was to find at least one Siren, and we found two. Unfortunately, the other Siren was in the third SUV and is out of reach for the moment. Your first mission will be to find out what this device is, who developed it, and what it can do. You find this out and report back to me. We will then devise a plan to make sure this device is not put to use. The rest of you were an added bonus. You will train until you are needed for an assignment. And you must be ready when that time comes."

INTERRUPTION

Jasmine was excited to know that she was now classified as a Dualist. In fact, the entire group was excited to see what new powers they possessed. But there was still confusion in the air. With a hint of uncertainty, Jasmine asked, "So you just expect us to go home and act as if nothing happened? You literally just took us from our friends and family, they will have questions about where we were."

The stranger announced, "Don't worry, everyone at the theatre has already been taken care of. At the conclusion of our recruitment, we had a Siren ensure everyone forgot about our extraction. Your friends and families will think you simply went home early."

"I see," said Owen. "Using your powers against others is ok when you do it?"

"This isn't something we wanted to do. As I mentioned before, our recruitment has been expedited as the threat levels have grown beyond comfort. The last four recruits were not Sirens and we were running out of time. A large group recruitment was required."

Maya asked, "What happened to the last four recruits?"

"Two out of four joined the Dualists."

"And the other two?"

"They were introduced to our Sirens, relieved of their powers, and returned home."

Olivia asked, "What do you mean, relieved of their powers? What did you do to them?"

"Listen, you must understand. The whole reason the Dualists exist is to stop wars before they happen. If you refuse to join us, then you are against us. We will not allow you to use your powers against us. Today, you will either join us, or return home an aural apathetic, completely uninterested in music."

"Who is even considering turning down this opportunity?" asked Jamie. "The chance to make a difference in this world, a chance to make it better."

"I'm not sure this is the best idea." After thinking for a short second, Malik continued, "I mean, how do you know the Sirens are planning to use this new device in a harmful way?"

The stranger answered, "That is the point of the research Jamie will do for us. If it is determined to be nothing, we will stand down and take no action."

Tanya asked, "And if it has the potential to do harm?"

"We must eliminate the device and its creator."

"Why must we eliminate the creator?" asked Max.

"In the past, we have tried to simply destroy the threat and use a Siren to erase the memory. However, evil people will maintain the path destined for them. If it is not the original threat, they will just think of the next threat and we will have gained nothing. Dualists have been around long enough to understand what needs to be done."

"And we are just supposed to follow the orders of a stranger?" asked Owen. "A bunch of masked strangers?"

The stranger replied, "My name is Miles Mack."

Emma's mouth nearly dropped to the floor when she heard that name. "Syncopation Sorcerer? Blessed with Instant Mastery, the ability of rapid learning and mastery of skills."

"Yes, Emma. I'm glad to know my reputation carries on."

"The last I heard, you were dead."

"Yes, another necessity. I could no longer continue hiding among everyone else with this threat lingering and growing like a disease. I faked my death so I could take on a full-time role. There is nothing I wouldn't do to save this world and I hope you all feel the same."

"I agree," added Max. "I mean think about it guys. We have been gifted with the abilities of dual genres! How amazing. We can learn how to control our new powers and use them to protect the world."

Maya disagreed. "How can you open your mouth to say protect the world, when you just heard him say he was willing to lie and cheat to get what he wants?"

"Oh come on!" Casey said. "We would only be eliminating threats who were trying to kill others anyway."

"We can't always know what people are going to do before they do them," said Emma. "What if they had intentions on doing something bad and then changed their minds? If you modify their ability to utilize music, we will never allow them to redeem themselves. We are not the judge and jury, give them a fair fight."

"I'm sorry," Max added, "if you make a device for mass destruction, you are more than likely to use that device for mass destruction. It is too late for you to change."

Just outside, Wyatt and the others were going over the plan to break in and rescue the group on the inside. They had no idea of the conversation going on between the captured and their captors. The idea of a person controlling two genres was still unknown to them. Since arriving, the group had been watching, studying, so meticulous, to ensure absolute victory.

"What if the others are under control of a Siren?" asked Jessica. "Ava, when you checked the vibes inside, no one appeared to be fighting back, right?"

"That's right, they were all just sitting there while one person was addressing them. But it didn't seem like they were being controlled, it seemed as if they were all talking to each other, like an active conversation. I just couldn't hear what they were saying. The building is made of stone and the vibrations are bouncing around too much for me to understand what is being said."

"That's probably intentional," said Wyatt, with his expertise in battle strategy. Wyatt crouched behind a rusted car on the edge of the abandoned warehouse's lot, scanning the building. His eyes narrowed as he now saw two guards patrolling the perimeter. He motioned for the others to gather closer. Jessica, Ava, Riley, Rachel, Oscar, and Grace moved in silently, their Beatlocks around their necks, ready for action.

"We've got two guards outside," Wyatt whispered, pointing toward the warehouse. "They'll be expecting something, but they don't know it's us."

Rachel glanced nervously at the building. "The others must be inside. They won't have their Beatlocks yet, so they'll be vulnerable."

Wyatt nodded. "That's our advantage. We have to move fast, get in before the strangers equip them or sway them to join their side."

Oscar, standing tall beside his sister, folded his arms. "We can't afford to charge in recklessly, though. The strangers will be armed and prepared. We need to work smart, not just hit hard."

Grace added, her soft voice filled with urgency, "I would like to try something. Earlier, I used light to blind them, I wonder if I could use light in a different way, if I could bend it. I think I could cloak us in a sense. I can make sure we aren't seen as we approach."

"Agreed," Wyatt said, rubbing his chin. "Grace, you cover us until we reach the entrance. After that, we go silent. Ava, your vibrations, can you still feel everyone inside?"

Ava closed her eyes, concentrating. Her fingers tapped lightly against the ground, sending subtle pulses of energy rippling through the earth. "I've got about a dozen distinct heartbeats inside," she whispered. "Two groups. One's closer to the entrance, probably guards. The other group is deeper in, further to the back. That's where the captives are."

Wyatt nodded, formulating the plan in his mind. "Here's what we'll do. Grace will keep us hidden until we're at the door. Then Ava will use her vibrations to disrupt any communications or alarms. Riley, you're on the metal locks and doors, quietly. Once we're in, we divide into two teams."

He drew a quick map on the dusty ground. "Oscar, Rachel, and I will handle the guards at the front. Rachel, if anyone isn't wearing Beatlocks, use your mind control to keep them quiet. Oscar, you and I will take down anyone who tries to fight."

Oscar gave a firm nod, his face set with determination. "We'll handle them."

Wyatt continued, "Jessica, Grace, and Riley, you head to the back to free the captives. Riley, you'll break the locks on their restraints. Jessica, cover them in case anyone shows up, and Grace, keep things discreet with your light powers."

Jessica clenched her fists, eager to get in the action. "We get in, we get the captives, and we get out before anyone knows what hit them."

Rachel's brow furrowed. "And what if some of the captives... turn on us? They've been held long enough for the strangers to make use of a Singing Siren on them. We don't know who's been swayed."

Wyatt looked her in the eye. "If they're wearing Beatlocks, they're enemies. But if they don't, we give them a chance to join us. Worst case, you'll stop them before they can do any damage. We won't risk hurting the innocent."

There was a tense silence as everyone processed the plan. Oscar broke it with a quiet, steady voice. "We stick to our strengths. Trust the plan and each other. Wyatt's right. The only way this works is if we stay smart and stay together."

Ava cracked her knuckles, releasing a subtle tremor. "Let's hope it's enough."

Wyatt stood up and glanced at the group. "We move now. Stick to the plan, and we bring them all home."

Ava quietly stopped Oscar and pointed to the first guard by the door. "That is the same person who kicked me! I want to take him on."

"Ava, there is more on the line than just redemption. This isn't the time to retaliate."

Ava, now deflated, was brought back to life as Oscar continued. "But don't worry sis, I will make sure he pays for what he did to my baby sister. Count on it."

SHOWDOWN

The group huddled close, listening as Wyatt laid out the plan. Rachel, Riley, Ava, Oscar, Jessica, and Grace waited silently, tension thick in the air. Grace shifted nervously, her mind racing. She had never attempted to cloak a group before. Brightening light around herself was one thing, but hiding all of them in pure darkness was a different challenge. Still, she knew it was the only way to get close without being seen.

"Grace," Wyatt said softly, turning to her. "Can you do it?"

Grace took a deep breath, nodding. "I... I think so."

She closed her eyes, focusing on the light around them. Her fingers twitched, feeling the familiar hum of energy, but this time she pushed herself further. Instead of multiplying the light and vanishing into the background, she pulled it in, warping and bending the existing light around the entire group. Her fingers moved in intricate patterns, and the air around them began to shift. The light from the nearby street lamps bent and twisted, molding around the group until a shroud of inky darkness enveloped them.

The air around them felt different, like they were suspended in an eerie, silent void. Grace opened her eyes and gasped softly. It had worked, better than she had ever imagined. The warehouse, the guards, the distant streetlights, they were all just outside of their reach, but the group was invisible, encased in darkness as though the night itself had swallowed them whole.

Jessica glanced around, wide-eyed. "Grace… this is amazing."

Wyatt looked around, impressed. "That's better than I expected. We're practically invisible."

Grace smiled faintly, though her hands trembled with the effort. "Let's hope I can hold it."

Wyatt gave her a reassuring nod. "We'll move quickly. Stay focused."

As the group began to move, Ava lagged behind for a moment, her thoughts racing. She had a strange, sudden feeling, something she couldn't quite shake. While they were invisible to the eye, their footsteps still echoed softly in the quiet night. What if the guards could hear them approaching?

Ava bit her lip, her mind spinning with the possibilities. She was always aware of vibrations. She could feel them, use them, sense the world through them. Just then, something clicked inside her, an idea she hadn't fully considered before.

"What if I can do more than just feel them?" she thought.

Without fully understanding how, Ava took the lead. Her steps became deliberate, each footfall sending a precise vibration through the ground. But this time, instead of broadcasting their presence, she countered the natural vibrations with her own. It was as if her steps created an opposite pulse that canceled out any sound they might have made.

The others followed her, and though they were stepping on gravel and debris, there was no sound. Not even the faintest crunch of a boot could be heard.

Wyatt noticed and leaned toward her. "Ava... what are you doing? How are you doing that?"

Ava blinked, surprised by her own actions. "I think... I stopped the sound of our footsteps. Now they can't hear us coming either! I can't let Grace do everything!"

Oscar, walking close behind, watched her with a mixture of awe and pride. "You're learning to cancel vibrations. Perfect balance."

Ava smiled a little, still not entirely sure how she had done it, but knowing it was something she could control now. "Let's go save the others!"

They moved through the lot, cloaked in Grace's darkness and Ava's silent steps, becoming more than just invisible, untraceable. The patrolling guards were oblivious as the shroud passed them by, keeping the team hidden. The tension in the air was thick as they neared the entrance of the warehouse.

Ava glanced at Wyatt as she prepared to scan the environment for security measures. She knelt down, placing her palms flat on the ground. A soft, barely perceptible hum vibrated through the concrete. After a few seconds, she opened her eyes. Ava confirmed there were no alarms. They were safe to make entry.

Wyatt gave a curt nod as if to say, "Good work." He then silently gave Riley the signal to unlock the doors.

Riley stepped forward, running his hands over the large metal door. He focused, feeling the material respond to his touch. With a flick of his wrist, the lock clicked open without a sound, and the door creaked slightly as it swung inward.

The team slipped inside, their movements still hidden within the darkness Grace maintained. The warehouse interior was dim, lit only by a few flickering lights high above. The sound of distant footsteps echoed from deeper within.

Wyatt motioned to split up as planned. "Oscar, Rachel, with me. The rest of you head for the captives. Stay sharp."

Jessica, Grace, and Riley nodded and moved toward the back of the warehouse, their figures disappearing into the shadows. Wyatt, Ava, Oscar, and Rachel crept toward the front, where they could hear low voices from the guards stationed near the entrance.

Rachel's pulse quickened. If the guards weren't wearing Beatlocks, she could take them down without a fight. Her powers pulsed at the edges of her consciousness, ready to be unleashed.

As they neared the guards, Wyatt whispered, "Rachel, can you sense anything?"

Rachel closed her eyes, reaching out with her mind. Two of the guards were close—too close to escape without confrontation. Her mental touch brushed against them, but she hit resistance. Both guards were wearing Beatlocks.

"No good," she whispered. "They've got Beatlocks. I can't control them."

Oscar and Wyatt exchanged glances. "We do this the hard way, then," Wyatt murmured.

Oscar's hand tightened into a fist. "Let's make it quick."

Wyatt nodded, signaling Oscar. With a deep breath, Oscar unleashed a sharp wave of vibrations toward the guards, the air humming as the force rippled out. The first guard staggered, thrown off balance as the vibrations hit him. Wyatt was on him in an instant, striking swiftly with a precise blow that sent the guard crumpling to the ground.

The second guard reacted quickly, raising his fists, but before he could strike, Oscar hit him with a second, more concentrated burst of vibrations, knocking the weapon from his hands. Wyatt moved in and silenced the guard with a swift kick to the neck, sending him sprawling across the floor.

Rachel exhaled softly, the tension easing as the guards were neutralized. "Nice work."

Oscar's expression remained serious as he glanced around. "We're not done yet."

Miles stood in the center of the main room, not too far from the heroes, his eyes narrowing as he sensed something shift in the warehouse. His intuition, sharpened by years of experience, could feel the sudden drop in the energy of his guards. Two had just gone down, taken out swiftly and quietly. He didn't know how, but he knew it was Wyatt and an unknown Bass Master. A small smirk curled his lips.

"Impressive," he muttered to himself.

He turned his attention back to the captives, the tension in the room thickening as he stepped forward. "We don't have much time," he said, his voice cold but commanding. "You all know why you're here. Each of you has a choice to make. I won't ask again," he said coldly. "Who will join the Dualists and claim your true potential?"

Jasmine was the first to speak, her voice steady and unyielding. "I won't join you. We're not your soldiers."

Beside her, Maya, Emma, Owen, and Olivia immediately nodded in agreement, their eyes defiant.

Miles studied them for a moment, his expression calm, but the dangerous gleam in his eyes made it clear their decision was unwise. He didn't need their approval. He only needed loyalty.

"Very well," he said coolly, turning his attention to the others.

Without hesitation, Casey, Jamie, and Max all stepped forward. Casey, with her jaw set in determination. "We're in." Jamie and Max quickly nodded, their loyalty unquestioning as they moved to stand beside Miles.

A satisfied smile crossed Miles's face. "You've made the right choice." He reached into a case beside him and pulled out three sets of Beatlocks, tossing them to Casey, Jamie, and Max. "Welcome to the Dualists."

As they hung the Beatlocks around their necks, the faint hum of power activated, and their auras shifted, attuned to the energy of their new alliance. Miles gestured to the far corners of the room. "Take up defensive positions. We're not alone."

Just then, the large steel doors at the far end of the warehouse creaked open, and the heroes slipped inside, still shrouded in Grace's fading cloak of darkness. The dim light from the overhead bulbs cast long shadows across the floor, but the moment they stepped inside, all eyes turned toward them. Grace dropped the cloak.

Wyatt was at the front, his stance steady, his eyes calculating. Behind him, Ava, Grace, Riley, Rachel, Jessica, and Oscar fanned out, prepared for anything.

Miles turned to face them, his smile widening. "Welcome," he said, his voice dripping with false warmth. "I've been expecting you."

Wyatt's eyes narrowed as he studied the room. His gaze flicked over the captives, noticing the tension in their bodies, and then locked onto Miles. There was no mistaking the man in front of him. He exuded power and confidence, the kind of leader who thrived on control.

"I have to admit," Miles continued, "I'm impressed. You fought your way through my guards, outsmarted the traps they set for you, and now you stand before me, stronger than before. I couldn't be more proud. At the same time, I am most displeased with those who were selected to orchestrate your recruitment." His voice dropped, taking on a more sinister edge. "But I must ask... what now? You've come to rescue your friends, haven't you?" He gestured to the captives, some of whom stood firm, while others looked visibly shaken.

Wyatt clenched his fists, but before he could respond, Miles raised a hand, stopping him. "Before we get to that, let me make you an offer."

The room seemed to hold its breath as Miles spoke.

"I represent a group, selectively known as the Dualists. However, we are more than just a group. We are the future, people with gifts like yours, like mine, who can manipulate sound, vibrations, and music itself in ways you've never imagined. But we're not just about power... we're about control. You could be part of something greater than you've ever known."

His eyes scanned over the band of determined juveniles, lingering on each of them for a moment. "Join me, and you can have everything. Power, influence, freedom. All I ask in return is one small thing."

Wyatt's jaw tightened. "What's the catch?"

Miles's smile returned, but it was colder now. "Erase the minds of those who refuse me. They've made their choice, but that doesn't mean they have to remember it. They can go back to their lives. We don't have to kill them. But they must not have the opportunity to oppose us."

The room fell silent. Jasmine, Maya, Emma, Owen, and Olivia stiffened, their expressions hardening.

Rachel took a step forward, her eyes blazing. "You can't be serious."

"Oh, but I am," Miles replied smoothly. "They turned me down. They don't want to be part of this world. So let's make sure they stay out of it."

Ava's breath hitched. She glanced at Wyatt, waiting for his signal. The group shifted, their stances defensive. They had prepared for this, but the stakes felt impossibly high.

Wyatt's eyes locked with Miles's. "We're not erasing anyone's mind."

Miles sighed dramatically. "A shame. I was hoping you'd see reason."

He motioned subtly with his hand, and the defeated guards from earlier began to rise, shaking off their earlier blows. From behind them, the two guards who had been stationed outside entered the warehouse, silently flanking the rescuers.

Now, the group found themselves surrounded. Miles and his new recruits in front of them, the guards closing in from behind. Wyatt glanced back, calculating their options. They were pinned down, with nowhere to run.

Miles's smile widened as he stepped forward, flanked by Casey, Jamie, and Max, all wearing their Beatlocks, their auras pulsing with newfound power. "It doesn't have to be this way," Miles said softly. "You can still join us, and we can end this without bloodshed."

Wyatt looked around, taking stock of their situation. They were outnumbered, and Miles had the upper hand. But surrendering wasn't an option.

Rachel took a step forward, her eyes fierce. "We're not erasing anyone's mind, and we're not joining you."

Oscar's voice rumbled from the back, steady and calm. "You may have numbers, but you underestimate us."

Miles raised an eyebrow. "Is that so?" His voice was calm, but the tension in the room was palpable. "Then I suppose we'll have to settle this the hard way."

A beat passed, then another, the silence electric. Everyone was prepared for battle.

Wyatt's voice cut through the tension, quiet but firm. "Ready yourselves."

Miles's grin turned predatory as the Dualists and the heroes squared off. "Let's see what you're made of." Miles looked past the group of heroes to the four Dualists in the back. "Fail me again, and the consequences will be severe." Shifting his attention to the new recruits, he continued,

"You three have not learned how to fight as a Dualist, and yet I expect you to assist in this victory."

As the tension reached its peak, Miles's grin widened, and in a blink, he vanished. No sound, no trace. Just gone.

"Where did he..." Jessica started, but before she could finish, the battle erupted.

Wyatt's instincts kicked in immediately. "Stay together! Defensive positions!" he barked, his tactical mind racing to cover all angles. His eyes darted across the room, assessing the battlefield. The Dualists, backed by Casey, Jamie, and Max, spread out with deadly intent, their Beatlocks thrumming with power. The captives stood behind the heroes, tense but ready to support.

Ava felt the vibrations of the approaching enemy, the subtle tremors in the ground beneath their feet. She didn't wait. Drawing on her vibrational powers, she sent out a shockwave that reverberated through the floor, destabilizing the Dualists' stance. It wasn't enough to knock them down, but it threw off their rhythm.

Casey, full of strength, charged toward Ava, her fist raised. But Ava was faster. Using the counter vibrations she had discovered earlier, she dampened the force of Casey's steps just enough to slow her approach. Casey felt as though she was running in quicksand. Ava sidestepped and retaliated with a vibrating pulse that rattled Casey's bones. Casey grunted, but her enhanced strength made her tough to bring down.

Wyatt, meanwhile, was calculating a strategy. "Oscar, target their Siren. She'll be the biggest threat. Rachel and Jessica, focus on mind control if they drop their Beatlocks. Riley, Grace, stay on the defensive with your powers. We need to protect the captives." His eyes flicked to Jasmine, Maya, Emma, Owen, and Olivia. "You five, stay close and stay ready."

Riley stepped forward, his hands outstretched as he locked onto Max, the Dualist with metal control. The two stared each other down, their powers beginning to clash. Metal pipes and crates in the warehouse rattled and lifted into the air as Riley and Max each tried to wrest control of the objects around them. Sparks flew as metal clashed against metal, the two evenly matched in their abilities.

Grace kept her focus on creating light distortions, bending it to cloak the group in shadows and making it harder for the Dualists to track their movements. Tanya, standing undecided on the battlefield, watched Grace carefully. She, too, could bend light, and her hesitation flickered as she considered joining in and helping her sister. The room darkened further as the light powers of the two women began to intermingle.

Rachel and Jessica stood back to back, scanning the battlefield for anyone who might drop their Beatlocks. "This is harder than I thought," Rachel muttered. Their powers couldn't penetrate the protective barrier the Beatlocks provided, but they were ready for the first opportunity.

Suddenly, Jamie advanced toward them, a smirk on her face. "You can't stop me," she taunted, armed with Beatlocks. But her focus wasn't on them. She turned her gaze toward the captives.

Olivia, sensing the emotional turbulence within Jamie, stepped forward. Her empathic ability immediately keyed into Jamie's mental state. She couldn't fully manipulate her through the Beatlocks, but she could still read her, understand her desires. "Jamie," she mouthed, her voice smooth and calculated. "You don't need to fight for them. Think about it. You don't really belong with the Dualists, do you?" Olivia made sure her lips moved in a smooth and fluid motion so Jamie, without her knowledge, could see exactly what she was saying. Even without hearing her words, Olivia was able to feed on Jamie's drive.

Jamie hesitated, just for a moment, but her resolve was firm. Olivia had planted a seed of doubt, but it wasn't enough. Not yet.

Malik, still undecided, stood off to the side, watching the chaos unfold. His wind powers stirred the air around him, but he hadn't yet chosen a side. His eyes darted between the heroes and the Dualists, conflicted.

Then, a figure materialized behind Oscar. Miles had reappeared, moving with eerie silence. Before Oscar could react, Miles unleashed a devastating sonic blast aimed directly at him. Oscar barely managed to throw up a vibrational shield, absorbing the worst of the impact, but he was thrown off balance. Miles grinned as he vanished again into the shadows.

"Unreal!" Oscar grunted as he pushed himself up. "He's fast, Wyatt!"

Wyatt's mind raced, searching for a way to track Miles, but then he saw Tanya finally make her move. She raised her hands, bending light to obscure Grace's cloak, revealing their position.

Grace, gritting her teeth, adjusted the light flow, fighting back to keep them concealed. But with Tanya's interference, it was a losing battle. "I can't hold it!" she shouted as the shadows around them flickered and faded.

Meanwhile, Maya stepped up beside Ava, their vibrational powers syncing in an instinctive bond. Together, they sent a shockwave through the floor, knocking back a few of the

Dualists who were trying to flank them. The synchronized vibrations created a powerful pulse that destabilized the enemies' footing, momentarily disorienting them.

"Nice teamwork," Ava muttered, her confidence growing.

Casey's eyes burned with determination as she spotted Wyatt amid the chaos. Her enhanced strength surged through her muscles, and she charged forward, the ground beneath her feet cracking from the force of her movement. Crates, debris, and metal shards were sent flying as she bulldozed her way toward him, her massive frame plowing through obstacles with terrifying ease. The fury in her wide arc of a punch was palpable. If it connected, Wyatt would be finished.

But Wyatt's eyes narrowed, his instincts and tactical mind working in overdrive. As Casey's fist whistled through the air, he threw himself to the side, narrowly avoiding the crushing blow. His mind raced, analyzing the situation in the blink of an eye. Casey wasn't just powerful—she was relentless, charging headfirst with brute force and little regard for finesse.

"Owen, I need you!" Wyatt called out as he rolled to his feet, his voice carrying over the clamor of battle.

Owen, already assessing the battlefield with the same razor-sharp mind as Wyatt, nodded. He understood Wyatt's plan without needing further explanation. Owen, always the quiet strategist, adjusted his stance and moved in sync with Wyatt. They had fought together long enough to communicate without words, each anticipating the other's movements with uncanny precision.

Casey snarled in frustration as she adjusted her course, pivoting with surprising agility for someone of her strength and size. She spotted Owen moving toward her, and her lips curled into a grin. "Think you can take me together?" she growled. "Good luck."

Her strength surged again, this time driving her forward with a speed that belied her bulk. She aimed a bone-shattering punch toward Owen's chest, intending to crush him with a single blow. But Owen had already anticipated her movement. As her fist came toward him, he sidestepped, slipping just out of reach. Wyatt, on the other side, mirrored the move perfectly.

Casey's momentum carried her forward, but Wyatt and Owen stayed just ahead of her, like hunters circling their prey. They knew they couldn't match her strength head on, but they didn't need to. Their plan wasn't to overpower her. It was to outthink her.

Wyatt feinted left, his body language suggesting he was preparing to strike. Casey took the bait, lunging toward him with a wide swing. But at the last moment, Wyatt ducked, and Owen was already moving. In perfect sync, Owen aimed a precise strike at the back of Casey's knee—a weak point, even for someone with enhanced strength. Casey faltered as her leg buckled slightly, throwing her off balance.

"Not so tough when you can't stand, are you?" Owen muttered under his breath, though he knew they weren't out of danger yet.

Casey roared in frustration, her eyes wild with fury. She swung her arm in a wide arc, trying to catch both Wyatt and Owen with a single backhanded strike. This time, her attack was more unpredictable, her sheer power making up for her momentary lack of balance.

Wyatt barely dodged, the force of the air from her swing brushing against his face. But instead of retreating, he used her overextension against her. As Casey's momentum carried her forward, Wyatt darted behind her, moving with calculated precision. He didn't aim for her head or her torso—those were fortified by her enhanced strength. Instead, he targeted her center of gravity.

With a swift motion, Wyatt swept his leg behind Casey's, timing the maneuver perfectly with Owen, who struck her from the side. The combined force was enough to send Casey stumbling forward, her massive form crashing into a stack of crates with a thunderous crash.

Casey roared as she pushed herself back to her feet, debris falling around her. Her eyes blazed with rage, but there was something else there now—confusion. She wasn't used to being outmaneuvered like this. Her strength had always been enough to bulldoze through any opposition, but now Wyatt and Owen were using her power against her.

"Come on!" Casey bellowed, slamming her fists into the ground and sending shockwaves through the floor. The impact cracked the concrete beneath her, and the shockwave sent Wyatt and Owen stumbling back, struggling to maintain their footing.

Wyatt's mind raced as he regained his balance. Casey's strength was becoming more unpredictable. They had to end this soon, or her raw power would overwhelm them both.

"Owen, we need to draw her into the open," Wyatt said, his voice low but urgent. He saw the flaw in Casey's approach now—her rage was blinding her. She was so focused on crushing them that she wasn't thinking tactically.

Owen nodded. "Got it."

They split up, circling Casey from opposite sides, forcing her to keep turning between them. Wyatt feinted again, drawing her attention, while Owen moved silently behind her. Casey, sensing the feint this time, didn't fall for it. Instead, she charged directly toward Wyatt, her fists raised for a powerful overhead strike.

But that was exactly what they wanted.

At the last second, Wyatt dove to the side, and Casey's fists slammed into the floor with earth-shattering force. The concrete beneath her shattered, sending shards flying in all directions. But Wyatt wasn't her target anymore. Owen was already behind her.

With perfect timing, Owen struck again, this time aiming for her lower back, where the strain of her enhanced strength was greatest. His blow landed with precision, sending a jolt through Casey's body and forcing her to collapse to one knee.

Wyatt seized the opportunity, moving in swiftly. He didn't aim to defeat her with brute force—that would be impossible. Instead, he focused on immobilizing her. He grabbed one of the heavy-duty straps from the nearby crates and looped it around her arm, pulling tight.

Casey growled and tried to break free, but Owen was already there, grabbing the other end of the strap and pulling in the opposite direction. Together, they managed to bind her arm, limiting her movement just enough to slow her down.

"You may be stronger than us," Wyatt said through gritted teeth as he and Owen worked together to keep her restrained, "but strength without control is just chaos."

Casey struggled against the bindings, her strength threatening to tear through the straps. But for the moment, she was contained—her raw power neutralized by Wyatt and Owen's precision and coordination. The battle wasn't over yet, but they had bought themselves time to turn the tide.

The room was filled with the clashing of powers, the hum of Beatlocks, and the shouts of battle. The heroes and the captives fought bravely, but they were still surrounded and had made little headway. Miles, Casey, Jamie, Max, and the Dualists formed a formidable force.

"Rachel, Jessica, be ready," Wyatt called as he saw an opportunity. One of the Dualists had lost focus, his Beatlock momentarily slipped off his ear.

Rachel's eyes lit up as she seized the chance. With a single thought, she dove into the mind of the unguarded Dualist, her power taking hold. "You're on our side, together we turn the tide!" she hollered, and the Dualist's expression went blank as he fell under her control.

As the battle raged on, Rachel's control over the Dualist tilted the scales, but only briefly. The intensity of the fight continued to rise, with each side refusing to give an inch. Amidst the chaos, Tanya, still undecided, found herself watching Grace struggle to maintain their cloaking in the face of her own interference. Her hesitation faded as she witnessed the camaraderie and resolve of the heroes. Something in her shifted, and she made her choice.

Tanya stepped forward, her hands glowing as she bent light toward the Dualists, blinding them for a split second. "I'm with you," she called to Grace, and in that moment, her light illuminated the battlefield, casting sharp shadows that danced around the room.

Malik stood at the edge of the conflict, his wind powers stirring the air with increasing intensity. His decision was made. He watched as Tanya stepped forward to side with the heroes, her light blinding the Dualists for a brief moment. Disappointment flickered in his eyes, but it quickly hardened into resolve.

He was done hesitating.

Malik's gaze locked onto Jasmine, who had been moving through the battlefield with eerie precision, her time-altering abilities keeping her a step ahead of everyone. Her movements seemed to blur in and out of sync with the flow of the battle, almost as if she existed in multiple moments at once.

"I've waited long enough," Malik muttered, his voice carried on a gust of wind as he thrust his hands forward. A sudden whirlwind surged from his palms, barreling toward Jasmine.

The wind hit her like a wall. But as Malik grinned, thinking he had caught her off guard, Jasmine's form flickered. Time slowed around her, and she sidestepped just before the full force of the wind could connect. Her figure seemed to blur as she shifted into another time pocket, only reappearing a few feet away.

"You think wind can control time?" Jasmine taunted, her voice almost echoing as she moved between moments, her perception out of sync with normal time. "You'll have to do better."

Malik's eyes narrowed. With a sharp twist of his wrist, the wind swirled into a vortex around him, lifting debris and dust off the ground. He thrust his hands outward again, launching a barrage of slicing winds in Jasmine's direction.

This time, Jasmine didn't dodge. Instead, she slowed the moment. To her, the winds moved sluggishly, giving her ample time to react. She weaved through the gusts with precise movements, as if dancing through a storm in slow motion.

But Malik wasn't about to let her control the tempo.

He clenched his fists, and suddenly the winds picked up speed, swirling violently in all directions. Jasmine felt the change immediately. Her control over time was still intact, but Malik's wind was now chaotic, moving unpredictably. Her altered moments no longer gave her as much of an advantage as before.

"You can manipulate time," Malik said, his voice booming through the storm he created. "But I control the air itself. You can't fight without breathing."

With a swift motion, he concentrated the wind, directing it to wrap around Jasmine in a tight spiral. The air around her began to thin, and Jasmine's chest tightened as her breathing became labored. Malik's smirk grew as he applied pressure, the wind constricting like an invisible coil.

Jasmine gasped, feeling her body slow as oxygen slipped away. But she wasn't out of options.

With a focused breath, she gathered her strength and reached deep into her powers, altering time in a different way. Instead of dodging or weaving, she bent the moment backward, reversing the constriction of the wind. For a split second, time reversed, and Malik's wind unwound itself just enough for her to slip free.

Malik's eyes widened in surprise as Jasmine reappeared, untouched by his attack. "What…?"

She smiled, catching her breath. "You're fast, Malik. But I can still turn back time."

Frustrated, Malik surged forward, riding the winds with incredible speed. He darted toward Jasmine, hands outstretched, wind slicing around him. Jasmine felt the pull of the air and slowed time once again, stepping aside—but this time, Malik anticipated her move.

Using the winds to propel himself even faster, Malik adjusted mid-charge, twisting in the air and launching a tornado-like strike at her. The whirlwind spun out in multiple directions, cutting off Jasmine's escape routes. She couldn't dodge them all.

Caught in the gusts, Jasmine stumbled as the wind threw her off balance. She skidded across the warehouse floor, her powers struggling to keep up with Malik's relentless onslaught. He had closed the distance between them, and now she was on the defensive.

"You can't outrun me forever!" Malik yelled, his winds building in force. He spun in a tight circle, creating a cyclone around them both, trapping Jasmine in a vortex of raging air.

But Jasmine, though winded, wasn't done yet.

In a moment of clarity, she tapped into her powers again—not to slow or reverse time, but to shift it. For just a few heartbeats, she sped up her personal timeline, allowing herself to move faster than normal.

With blinding speed, Jasmine shot forward, her accelerated state catching Malik off guard. She darted through the windstorm, her fist connecting with Malik's midsection before he could react. The blow knocked the wind out of him—quite literally. Malik gasped as he staggered back, his winds faltering.

Jasmine, still in her heightened state, moved in again, delivering a series of quick strikes that pushed Malik further back. Each hit was timed perfectly, landing in moments when Malik's defenses were down.

But her acceleration came with a cost. She couldn't sustain it for long. Time snapped back to normal, and Jasmine felt the strain on her body as her powers ebbed. She slowed, her breath heavy, giving Malik a chance to recover.

"You're good," Malik panted, wiping the sweat from his brow. "But I'm not out yet."

With a fierce gust of wind, he created distance between them, and the battle continued.

Riley, locked in a fierce battle with Max, barely dodged the incoming gust. Metal clanged around them as their powers collided, the air charged with energy. Both fought for dominance, their control over the scrap metal in the room clashing in a brutal tug of war.

"Give it up, Riley!" Max growled, sweat beading on his forehead. His Beatlocks pulsed with energy, feeding his powers.

"Not a chance!" Riley shot back, his muscles straining as he summoned more force, every piece of metal in the warehouse vibrating with potential. Their powers crackled in the air, sparks flying as metal twisted and clanged against each other, creating a barrier between the rest of the fighters.

The intensity of their duel reached a breaking point. Riley's heart pounded, his veins surging with adrenaline. His body screamed with effort, but something deep inside him clicked, his powers igniting in ways he hadn't tapped into before. A rush of energy, raw and unbridled, coursed through him. His vision sharpened, muscles tightened, and suddenly everything seemed to slow down around him.

Adrenaline Surge.

With a roar, Riley tore through Max's defenses, the metal in the room whipping violently under his control. His speed increased, and before Max could react, Riley was on him. A flurry of strikes, impossibly fast and powerful, landed in quick succession, and Max was forced to protect himself, the metal he once controlled now wrapping around him, constricting.

"No!" Max grunted, trying to fight back, but Riley's Adrenaline Surge overwhelmed him. The metal bindings tightened around Max's body, locking him in place. With one final push, Riley sent Max crashing into a pile of debris, immobilized.

As the battle raged on, Wyatt realized they couldn't win without empowering the captives. But the Beatlocks were still in Miles's possession, locked in a reinforced case on a platform near the center of the room, far beyond easy reach. The situation was growing dire. The Dualists pressed in from all sides, and the heroes were being pushed back, their defenses faltering.

Then, Riley's Adrenaline Surge reached its peak. His eyes locked onto the case, and without hesitation, he used the surrounding metal debris to form a barrier between the Dualists and the captives. With a burst of speed, Riley launched himself toward the platform, moving faster than anyone could track. Metal clashed violently around him as Max desperately tried to stop him, but Riley's surge had taken full control.

With a powerful yank, Riley tore the case free from its lock and sent it flying through the air toward the captives. "Catch it!" he shouted, his voice amplified by the adrenaline pumping through him.

Jasmine, using her time-slowing ability, stepped forward in slow motion, guiding the case gently through the air as it glided toward the captives. Time around her returned to normal as the case landed safely in Owen's hands.

Owen opened the case, revealing the Beatlocks inside. Without missing a beat, Jasmine, Maya, Emma, and Olivia reached in and grabbed their sets, the faint hum of power immediately resonating with each of them. The transformation was instant. Their auras shifted as the Beatlocks attuned to their unique gifts, amplifying the abilities they had only begun to understand.

Jasmine's eyes sparkled with newfound control as she slowed the Dualists' movements even more effectively, giving her group precious moments to regroup. Olivia's empathic powers intensified, allowing her to sense the emotional shifts not only within the Dualists but among her friends, creating a tighter synergy between them.

Maya, syncing her Beatlocks with Ava, doubled the frequency of their vibrations, creating shockwaves so powerful they cracked the floor beneath the Dualists. The synchronized pulse destabilized the opposition, making it harder for them to gain ground.

As the captives activated their Beatlocks, the tide of the battle shifted. The group now stood on equal footing with the Dualists, their powers unleashed in full force.

The sheer force of Riley's power stunned both sides. For a brief moment, the battle froze.

"Now's our chance!" Wyatt shouted.

Tanya, her light still blazing, gave a determined nod. "I'll blind them," she said, raising her arms. A blinding flash exploded across the room, and the Dualists shielded their eyes, momentarily disoriented.

Grace, seizing the moment, stepped forward. Drawing from her newfound abilities, she cloaked the group in a shroud of impenetrable darkness, wrapping them in shadow. The combined effect of Tanya's light and Grace's darkness created an intense visual dissonance, concealing the heroes in a pocket of nothingness, completely invisible as they moved swiftly toward the exit.

Oscar, limping but determined, helped guide the captives through the dark. Jasmine slowed time around them, enhancing their movements, ensuring no one lagged behind.

As the group slipped away, Wyatt glanced back, his eyes locking with Miles, who had reappeared amidst the chaos. Miles's expression was one of amusement, though the tension in his eyes revealed his frustration. "This isn't over," he called after them, his voice echoing through the warehouse.

Wyatt didn't respond. They had achieved their goal. They had escaped. But this was far from over.

Together, cloaked in shadows, the heroes vanished into the night, leaving behind the chaos and the lingering tension of a battle only just begun.

REDEMPTION

The heroes successfully made their escape, slipping into the safety of the night. Once they were far enough from the warehouse, the group huddled together in an alley, breathing heavily from the intensity of the battle. It was clear they needed to regroup, but also that they couldn't stay together indefinitely.

"We need to stay in contact," Wyatt said, wiping the sweat from his brow. "Things are only going to get more complicated from here. I have no idea what the Dualists plan on doing now that we have escaped. For now, let's keep what happened between us. Based on what Miles said, it is possible there are Dualists throughout each of our communities. We don't know who to trust."

The others nodded in agreement. One by one, they exchanged numbers, ensuring they could reach out when needed.

Ava sighed, glancing at Riley. "You okay, kid? You really pushed yourself back there."

Riley gave a weak smile, still catching his breath. "Yeah, just… exhausted. The adrenaline surge really took it out of me."

Grace, standing nearby, spoke up. "Tanya and I can walk him home. Make sure he gets back safely."

"Thanks, Grace," Wyatt said, giving her a nod of appreciation. "We'll need to lay low for a while. Everyone, go your separate ways but keep your beatlocks on you at all times!"

One by one, the group dispersed into the night. Grace, Tanya, and Riley began their walk, moving toward Riley's neighborhood. They talked quietly along the way, the adrenaline of the battle still buzzing in their veins.

"Riley, you were amazing back there," Tanya said, a small smile forming on her lips. "I've never seen anyone control metal like that. You've got real talent."

Riley blushed slightly. "Thanks. I just— I couldn't let Max get the better of me."

As they approached Tanya and Grace's house, the two sisters exchanged glances. "Let's fill in Mom and Dad,"

Grace said, and they guided Riley inside. Their parents were waiting, worried looks on their faces.

"What's going on?" their father asked, standing from the couch. "Where have you been? And why does Riley look like he's been in a war zone?"

Grace and Tanya began portraying the cover story they devised during their walk. They explained how Riley was practicing for his advanced placement test when he unlocked his adrenaline surge but underestimated the toll it would have on his body. Their parents listened, concern etched across their faces as they offered to make Riley a nice warm dinner so he could rest up before he headed home.

Riley was surprised at this. Other genres were not this nice to people who were outside of their musical taste. His exhausted mind let the thought escape him as he wrote it off. Gospel were usually nice people, so it was par for the course.

At the same time, back at the warehouse, Miles stood before the Dualists and the new recruits, his expression dark with frustration. He paced back and forth, his usual calm demeanor slipping.

"I cannot believe," Miles began, his voice low and cold, "that you let them slip away. All of you, together, with all your powers, and you couldn't even handle a small group."

Casey, Jamie, and Max exchanged glances, clearly uncomfortable. Max, still sore from his defeat at Riley's hands, clenched his fists. "It's not like we didn't try! But where were the rest of the Dualists? They barely did anything!"

One of the Dualists, arms crossed and unimpressed, shot back, "You recruits ran in like headless chickens. No discipline. You muddied the battlefield and ruined any chance of a coordinated strategy."

"That's crap!" Casey growled, her enhanced strength making her presence intimidating. "If you'd actually fought, we could've won."

The argument escalated, voices rising. Then, the group heard a loud crash, forcing them into defensive positions. Miles didn't bother looking, very much aware, already knowing what the noise was. The others turned to see the Dualist Rachel had mind-controlled slamming into a wall, still trying to follow the heroes' last command. His body crumpled to the ground, the beatlocks slipping off his head.

Miles sneered in disgust. "Jamie, free him."

With a roll of her eyes, Jamie stepped forward and placed her hand on the guard's forehead, her powers severing the mental hold Rachel had placed on him. The guard blinked rapidly, confused and disoriented.

"Ugh. Pathetic," Miles spat, shaking his head. "You'll be lucky if I let you clean this place, let alone train in it."

He turned to address the entire group, his patience visibly wearing thin. "Stay here. I'll be assigning a team leader soon. Someone capable. Someone who knows how to take control of this mess. They'll arrive shortly to handle things."

With that, Miles vanished once more, leaving the Dualists and recruits in the dimly lit warehouse. A tense silence fell over the group.

One of the guards, now free from Rachel's influence, broke the silence. "We can't just sit here. We should go after them, find those kids and bring them back. Imagine how impressed Miles would be."

Another guard, this one standing beside him, nodded in agreement. "Yeah, Kaden's right, he's not gonna wait forever. If we capture them, we'll be back in his good books."

But one of the more disciplined Dualists interjected. "No. We were told to wait here. I intend to follow those orders. Kaden, Austin, you two should do everything in your power not to upset him again. If you want to risk it all, I won't stand in your way. Success will indeed win you some brownie points. However, failure will surely get your abilities muted! I would wait here if I were you two."

Kaden and Austin weren't having it. "Forget that," Kaden said. "This is our shot." Without waiting for approval, the two Dualists sprinted toward the exit, ignoring the protests of their comrades.

As the two reckless Dualists caught up with their target, they found the heroes had already disbanded. All that remained were Grace, Tanya, their parents, and Riley, who was barely keeping himself upright, his energy completely drained.

The two Dualists exchanged glances, sensing an opportunity. "Looks like we found a few glow sticks. The Titan looks too tired to fight, we can take them."

Austin agreed, "I'll take on the sisters, you get the parents?"

Kaden agreed, and the two took battle positions on opposite ends of the house. Kaden knew this was his opportunity to shine. If he was able to bring back three of the five captives, Miles would forgive his previous failures.

With this in mind, he began to strategize. He knew he was about to take on the parents of two amateur Luminescent Believers. Their powers were light-based. Kaden was a Dualist who studied under Rocking Resilience and the Empathetic Harmonizers. Kaden did not want to lose this battle and knew he must execute flawlessly.

Austin, on the other hand, looked up to Kaden. They had been best friends since they were young. Austin's only drive was to help Kaden. This has proven to be an extremely good muse, as Austin is arguably a better Dualist than Kaden. Austin, however, did not want to outshine his friend, so he kept his powers in check in order to keep their friendship alive. Austin had been studying under the Empathetic Harmonizers and the Lyrical Windweavers.

This was not the first time the two Dualists had taken on a mission together. They always started the same: they acted as if jazz was the only music ability they had unless they were losing the battle. Switching genres mid-battle, without fail, completely disoriented their opponents, who now had to think of a new strategy. This gave the two Dualists time to overwhelm their opponents and claim victory. It was the first strategy learned when they became Dualists, and they had not ventured to learn any others. As Kaden always said, "If it ain't broke, don't fix it!"

As Kaden and Austin stealthily approached Grace's home, their eyes locked on their targets. Kaden's gaze settled on

Grace's parents, assuming them to be intermediate Luminescent Believers. He believed they only possessed defensive abilities: generating light for communication, creating shields, and calming those around them—nothing offensive. Confident, Kaden smirked. He would wrap this up quickly.

At the same time, Austin turned his focus toward Grace and Tanya. They had only displayed beginner-level abilities so far, just bursts of bright light, nothing more. He was convinced that was the full extent of their power. "This'll be easy," Austin muttered as he adjusted his beatlocks.

Kaden, feeling the pulse of jazz music through his beatlocks, was the first to strike. He activated his elasticity, limbs stretching and coiling like serpents. His hands shot out and wrapped around Grace's mom and dad, binding them tight. His goal was simple: prevent them from using their light-based powers by physically restraining them.

With a grin, Kaden quickly switched from jazz to rock, triggering his ability, Adversity Absorption. The energy Grace's parents used in their struggle was siphoned into him, converting into pure strength. Kaden felt a surge of power course through his body, muscles bulging as he tightened his grip.

But in his overconfidence, he made a mistake. His rapid shift between music genres caught the attention of Grace's parents, who immediately noticed the change in energy flow. "There are two different powers at play here," Grace's father whispered to his wife, his eyes narrowing as he assessed the situation.

Meanwhile, Austin attacked. His elastic limbs snapped out toward Grace and Tanya, his beatlocks thrumming with jazz. His hands stretched, ready to ensnare the sisters just like Kaden had with their parents. Riley, despite being weakened from the earlier battle, saw the incoming threat and leaped to help. But Austin swatted him away with a casual flick of his foot, sending Riley sprawling to the ground.

"Riley!" Grace shouted, but her attention was immediately pulled back as Austin's hands closed in on her and Tanya.

Just as it seemed Kaden's plan was working flawlessly, Grace's parents revealed their true power. They weren't intermediate Luminescent Believers—they were experts. With a determined look, they activated their ultimate technique: Purifying Aura.

A soft glow surrounded Grace's mom and dad, enveloping them in a radiant, soothing light. Kaden's mind, once sharp and focused on capturing them, began to blur. The Purifying Aura fostered a deep sense of peace, calming his aggression and stopping his attack in its tracks. His elastic grip loosened involuntarily as the aura washed over him, breaking his focus.

Austin, now the sole attacker, realized Kaden was out of commission and switched tactics. He quickly shifted his beatlocks to hip-hop, summoning wind manipulation. With a sharp motion of his hand, he altered the air density around Grace's parents. The wind around them thickened, growing heavy, and the very air they breathed became oppressive. The weight pressed down on them, and they struggled to remain upright.

The Purifying Aura flickered, unable to sustain itself under the immense pressure of Austin's wind manipulation. Kaden, still recovering from the effects of the aura, began to regain his senses. Things looked grim for Grace and Tanya.

Suddenly, Grace's father acted. "Lightbringer's Resurgence!" he called out, his hands glowing with an intense, healing light. The light shot toward Riley, who lay on the ground, battered and weakened. The moment it touched him, Riley's strength was restored, his exhaustion wiped away in an instant.

Riley sprang to his feet, his eyes blazing with determination. Drawing on his metal-manipulating abilities, he reached deep beneath the earth, ripping pipes from underground. The metal erupted from the ground, snaking through the air as Riley's power surged. With a mighty gesture, he wrapped the pipes around both Kaden and Austin, binding them tightly.

The air around Grace's parents returned to normal as Austin's wind control faltered. But even in his restrained state, Austin wasn't done yet. He puffed his cheeks and fired sharp wind darts from his mouth, aiming at the group.

"Not today!" Grace shouted, her hands glowing with light. She and Tanya unleashed a blinding flash of light directly at Austin, momentarily disorienting him. While Austin was blinded, Riley acted fast. He reached out with his powers and yanked the beatlocks from Austin's head, rendering him powerless.

On the other side, Grace's parents swiftly moved to Kaden, whose strength had been sapped by Riley's metal bindings and their Purifying Aura. With a quick motion, they removed Kaden's beatlocks, neutralizing him as well.

The battle was over. Kaden and Austin lay defeated, their powers stripped away. Grace, Tanya, Riley, and their parents stood victorious, the air around them returning to calm.

"Thanks for saving me," Riley said, still catching his breath.

Grace's father smiled, his calming aura fading. "We're all in this together. Now let's make sure these two don't cause any more trouble."

Back at the warehouse, the tension was thick as the new leader arrived. He strode in confidently, his eyes sweeping over the wreckage from the failed mission. The Dualists and new recruits stood in scattered clusters, waiting for him to speak. His presence alone commanded attention, and it was clear he was not someone to be taken lightly.

"I've been appointed to run the next operation," the new leader said, his voice calm but firm as he examined the damaged equipment and debris strewn across the room. "Miles gave me a debrief of what happened with this botched mission. But even in failure, we gained some intel."

The Dualists and recruits exchanged nervous glances. No one was sure where this was going.

The leader turned slightly, his back still facing them as he continued. "Did any of you notice anything strange about two of the captives during the incident?"

There was silence. The Dualists, Jamie, Casey, and Max, as well as the new recruits, looked at each other, confusion in their eyes. None of them spoke up.

The leader's expression didn't change. He had expected as much. "I didn't think you would have noticed," he said quietly, almost to himself. Then, louder, "Rachel, the one who managed to take control of a Dualist... she wasn't wearing beatlocks."

The air in the warehouse shifted. Jasmine, standing toward the back of the group, was the first to react. "She shouldn't have been able to use her abilities without beatlocks on," Jasmine said slowly, as if the realization was just dawning on her.

The leader turned slightly, acknowledging her with a nod. "You must be Jasmine, the Singing Siren." His voice was low, almost calculating. "And yes, you're correct. That alone changes the game."

He finally turned to face the entire group, his sharp eyes scanning them as if he already knew more than he was letting on. "Where are Kaden and Austin?"

Taz, one of the more experienced Dualists, shifted uncomfortably before speaking. "They went after the ones who escaped... against Miles' orders," he admitted reluctantly.

The other Dualist, Dame, added with a scowl, "They thought they could bring them back. Their last transmission said they'd found Grace, Tanya, and Riley. They were at the residence of the Luminescent Believers."

At the mention of the Luminescent Believers, the new leader's eyes narrowed, a flicker of concern crossing his face. "Were their parents home?" he asked, his tone sharper now, as if the stakes had just risen.

Taz and Dame exchanged uncertain glances before Taz finally nodded. "Yes."

The new leader's jaw clenched for a brief moment before he composed himself. "If their parents are involved, Kaden and Austin are walking into something they're not prepared for." His eyes darkened. "Those aren't any run-of-the-mill LBs. They're experts."

The weight of his words sank into the room, and the Dualists stiffened, realizing the gravity of the situation. Dame, sensing the urgency, looked at the group and barked, "Ready up! We move now!"

As the group rushed to prepare, the new leader lingered for a moment, his thoughts racing. He hadn't expected a complication this early on, but this mission wasn't just about capturing runaways anymore. Something bigger was at play, and Rachel's ability to use her powers without beatlocks only deepened the mystery. They had to act fast. He knew this mission had just become far more complicated than any of them had anticipated. And if Kaden and Austin had failed, it was only the beginning.

The new leader's squad moved swiftly through the night, their footsteps nearly silent as they closed in on the last known location of Kaden and Austin. The tension among the group was palpable, but no one dared to question the new leader's command. As they approached, they spotted the two captured Dualists, bound and restrained by the Luminescent Believers.

Taz, full of adrenaline, instinctively began to move forward. "We have to get them—"

The leader's hand shot out, stopping him cold. "This is a command," the leader said sharply, his tone leaving no room for debate. "Stay here until I return. Under no circumstances do you engage in battle."

Taz froze, startled by the leader's intensity. Before anyone could protest, the leader equipped his beatlocks. In an instant, he was gone, a blur of movement so fast it left the squad in stunned silence. The leader stopped no less than 75 feet ahead, standing right between the escaped captives and the Luminescent Believers, his form calm and composed.

Grace, Tanya, Riley, and the parents immediately noticed him. The man's sudden appearance sent a jolt through them. "Who are you?!" Grace demanded, her voice wavering between fear and defiance.

The leader didn't respond. Instead, he activated his Time Twister abilities, casting Time-Warp Aura. An eerie energy enveloped the group, and the world around them seemed to slow to a crawl. Grace and the others moved as though trapped in molasses, their motions sluggish, their voices drawn out into incomprehensible whispers. To them, everything felt like a dream, slow and distorted, but to the leader, it was nothing more than a controlled manipulation of time.

Walking with precision, the leader approached Grace, moving 50 times faster than those caught in his aura. He leaned in close, whispering something into her ear, too quiet for anyone else to hear.

Grace's eyes widened, her pupils dilating with shock, but her body was unable to react. The leader pulled back and strode over to where Austin lay bound. With a wave of his hand, he activated Screwed Reality Shift, a technique that allowed him to access alternate realities. The metal pipes that held Austin became soft and malleable, bending like rubber in his grip. Effortlessly, the leader freed Austin.

Next, he moved to Kaden, repeating the process and releasing him as well. Kaden stood, fury burning in his eyes, but his humiliation from being captured clouded his judgment. Without hesitation, he started to march toward Grace's parents, anger blazing in his every step.

"Enough," the leader's voice cut through the air like a blade, stopping Kaden in his tracks. "Follow me."

For a moment, Kaden hesitated, frustration etched into his face. But something in the leader's tone or presence made him obey. He turned away from the battle, falling in line behind the leader.

The leader led Kaden and Austin back toward the rest of the Dualists. Once they were a safe distance away from the scene, he turned to the squad, his eyes cold and unreadable. Without a word, they departed into the shadows, vanishing as quickly as they had come.

Back at the Luminescent Believers' residence, the time-distorting aura finally dissipated. Grace, Tanya, Riley, and the parents were freed, able to move normally again. Relief washed over them, but something was wrong. Grace's body trembled, her face pale.

"Grace?" her father asked, concern evident in his voice as he stepped toward her.

But Grace couldn't respond. Instead, she collapsed to her knees, her chest heaving as sobs wracked her body. Tears streamed down her face as she cried, unable to contain the overwhelming emotions that had consumed her. The weight of whatever the leader had whispered to her bore down like an unbearable burden.

Her father quickly knelt beside her, placing a comforting hand on her shoulder. "What did he say to you?" he asked, his voice gentle but filled with urgency.

Grace shook her head, unable to speak through the tears, her entire body shuddering. Whatever the leader had said, it had shaken her to her core.

The rest of the group looked on in worried silence, the eerie calm of the night settling back in. But the feeling of unease lingered, heavy and oppressive, as if the battle they had just survived was only the beginning of something far worse.

The chapter ended not with victory, but with the unsettling knowledge that the enemy was more dangerous, and more mysterious, than any of them had realized.

Bass Master's Power Set

This ranking considers the complexity, versatility, and potential impact of each ability in battle scenarios, with Novice powers being foundational, Intermediate powers showing more advanced control, and Expert powers demonstrating mastery over the vibrational spectrum.

Novice

Vibrational Perception: Resonance Awareness

Enhanced senses that allow users to perceive their surroundings through vibrations. This includes detecting hidden objects, discerning materials, or even sensing the emotional state of others through their vibrational frequencies.

Vibro-Enhanced Reflexes: Hyper-Reflex Harmonics

Increased reaction speed by attuning the user's nervous system to vibrational stimuli, allowing for heightened reflexes and swift responses to threats.

Vibrational Creation: Vibrogenesis

Users can generate vibrations from their body or surrounding environment, creating powerful shockwaves with varying frequencies. These shockwaves can be harnessed for offensive or defensive purposes.

Vibrational Manipulation: Resonance Control

The ability to manipulate the frequency, intensity, and direction of vibrations. Users can fine-tune vibrations to shatter objects, create sonic barriers, or induce controlled earthquakes.

Vibrational Camouflage: Inaudible Presence

The ability to manipulate one's own vibrational frequency to become invisible to both the naked eye and conventional detection methods, making the user effectively unseen and unheard.

Vibration Absorption: Harmonic Absorption

The power to absorb and nullify external vibrations, rendering the user immune to sonic attacks, seismic disturbances, or any harmful vibrations. This absorption can also empower the user, enhancing their abilities.

Expert

Sonic Constructs: Sonic Constructs

Transforming vibrations into solid, tangible constructs such as weapons, shields, or platforms. The constructs retain the vibrational properties, adding an extra layer of versatility to the user's abilities.

Vibrokinetic Flight: Aero-Vibration

Users can fly by emitting vibrations beneath them, essentially riding shockwaves as a form of propulsion. The speed and maneuverability depend on the user's mastery of this skill.

Healing Harmonics: Sonic Restoration

The power to heal oneself or others by mending molecular structures through harmonic vibrations. This ability allows users to accelerate the natural healing process or even regenerate tissues.

Vibro-Telepathy: Vibrational Communication

Transmitting messages or thoughts through vibrations, creating a unique form of telepathy that operates on vibrational frequencies. This enables secure communication without conventional means.

Dimensional Resonance: Interdimensional Travel

Mastery over vibrations allows users to create portals or rifts between dimensions by attuning vibrations to the unique frequencies of different realities. This skill requires precision to navigate safely.

Singing Siren's Power Set

These powers draw inspiration from the infectious and captivating nature of Pop music, providing individuals with the charisma and influential abilities to connect with others, captivate audiences, and navigate social situations with charm and popularity.

Novice

Pop Pulse Projection

Emit pulses of energetic charisma that affect the emotions of those nearby. This power allows individuals to create a positive and uplifting vibe, elevating the mood in any environment.

Sonic Charisma

The power to emit a captivating aura through the resonance of pop music. Individuals can draw attention, exude charm, and easily establish connections with those around them.

Intermediate

Social Harmony Manipulation

The ability to influence and harmonize social dynamics. Individuals can navigate through various social circles with ease, promoting unity and understanding while fostering a positive and inclusive atmosphere.

Celestial Magnetism

Draw people towards them like planets orbiting a star. This power enhances the individual's attractiveness and magnetism, making them the center of attention in social situations.

Charm Infusion

Infuse objects or words with charm, creating items or phrases that have an irresistible influence on those who encounter them. This power is especially effective in persuasion and negotiation.

EXPERT

Pop Star Presence

Adopt a dazzling and influential persona reminiscent of pop stars. Individuals can command attention, exude confidence, and inspire admiration, making them natural leaders in social settings.

Euphoric Empathy

The ability to deeply understand the emotions of others and respond with empathetic charm. Individuals can connect with people on a personal level, making them a source of comfort and support.

Audience Adoration

Command the adoration and loyalty of crowds. This power allows individuals to effortlessly captivate audiences, whether in a public speech, performance, or casual interaction.

Societal Uplift

Channel the energy of pop music to uplift and inspire communities. Individuals can use their charismatic influence to promote positive change, unity, and cooperation on a larger scale.

Instant Rapport

Establish instant rapport and connection with individuals from diverse backgrounds. This power enables individuals to quickly build trust, understanding, and camaraderie with anyone they encounter.

METAL TITANS POWER SET

These powers collectively reflect the strength, resilience, and intensity associated with metal music, providing a unique and dynamic set of abilities for those who possess this extraordinary gift.

NOVICE

Metal Detection
The ability to sense and detect metal objects or disturbances in the environment. This power aids in situational awareness, providing an advantage in combat or survival scenarios.

Epic Resonance
The ability to create awe-inspiring and empowering musical compositions on the spot, capable of influencing emotions and inspiring courage in those who hear it. This power can be a source of leadership and motivation for groups.

INTERMEDIATE

Sonic Empowerment
The power to share the benefits of metal music with others. By creating a sonic field of empowerment, individuals can temporarily boost the physical and mental strength of allies within the vicinity.

Magnetic Manipulation
Control over magnetic fields, inspired by the magnetic nature of metal. This power allows individuals to manipulate metal objects, create magnetic barriers, or even levitate metallic substances.

Rhythmic Healing
Utilizing the healing properties of metal music, individuals can accelerate their own healing process or heal others by creating a rhythmic resonance that promotes cellular regeneration and recovery.

Adrenaline Surge
The capacity to induce a controlled adrenaline rush, boosting physical strength, speed, and endurance. This power can be activated during intense situations, providing a temporary but significant enhancement of physical abilities.

EXPERT

Sonic Resilience

The power to absorb and channel the energy from metal music, converting it into a personal force field that provides enhanced physical and mental resilience. This shield can withstand various forms of attacks and stress.

Mind of Steel

Mental fortitude that makes the individual impervious to psychological attacks. This power allows for unwavering focus, resilience against mental manipulation, and the ability to maintain clarity under stress.

Fury Manifestation

Ability to manifest the intense emotions conveyed in metal music into a physical force. This power allows individuals to unleash waves of powerful energy, causing disruptions in the environment and repelling adversaries.

Metal Affinity

A heightened connection to metal elements, granting control over metals in the vicinity. This power enables manipulation of metal objects, creating weapons or defensive structures on demand.

About the Author

The O'Neal Family

Hello everyone! First of all, thank you so much for buying one of my books. I am a new author and I really look forward to making more books for you all to enjoy. The reason I started writing was for my daughter. She absolutely loves reading books. Like her father, she loves reading comic books. We read all of the age appropriate books but as she got older and her intelligence rose off the charts, I had a hard time finding something that was interesting for her and still age appropriate. She and I started writing little shorts stories that had us laughing until our stomachs were sore. Then my wife suggested that we actually start making some books together and here we are. I hope you enjoy!

www.ingramcontent.com/pod-product-compliance
Lightning Source LLC
Chambersburg PA
CBHW071521100726
47908CB00004B/1245